"Drake. I need you to come and look at some bones."

"Your bones?" He yawned through the phone.

This was rather heavy-handed, but since he'd obviously not had his morning espresso, I forgave him. "No. These bones are dead. Very dead, from the look of things."

"Human bones? Really?" He sounded more awake.

"I don't know." I looked at the cranium. It wasn't a whole skull—just a bowl-shaped curve about the size of the back of my head. "But could be, I guess."

He yawned again. "Where are you, anyway?"

"I'm at Bridget's, remember? You're supposed to be taking care of Barker for me while I take care of things here."

"Right." I could hear various rustling noises. "Okay," he said, after a moment. "I've got my glasses on. I'll get dressed and bring Barker over. Don't let the boys stir up the bones any more than they already have."

By Lora Roberts
Published by Fawcett Books:

MURDER IN A NICE NEIGHBORHOOD
MURDER IN THE MARKETPLACE
MURDER MILE HIGH
MURDER BONE BY BONE

MURDER BONE BY BONE

Lora Roberts

Lora Roberts

*For Linda — sure
hope your ankle
bone's connected ...*

FAWCETT GOLD MEDAL • NEW YORK

A Fawcett Gold Medal Book
Published by Ballantine Books
Copyright © 1997 by Lora Roberts Smith

Library of Congress Catalog Card Number: 96-90736

ISBN 0-449-14946-3

Manufactured in the United States of America

First Edition: March 1997

10 9 8 7 6 5 4 3 2

For Barbara Dicks, one of the great editors of the world.
And for Ruth Cohen, one of the great agents.
Thanks, ladies.

I had help with the forensic aspects of this book from Chuck Cecil of the San Francisco Medical Examiner's office. Any mistakes are mine, arising from the dictates of my plot.

I have taken great liberties with Stanford University, creating my own version of their archaeology program, staffing it with my imagined people, and making their procedures fit my needs. In other words, I made it all up. Same with the Palo Alto Public Works department and with everybody else in the book. Any similarities to real life mean that the reader has a good imagination, too.

MURDER
BONE BY BONE

1

THROUGH the window over the diaper table, in the backyard, I could see them hitting.

I tried to hurry with diapering Moira, but she kept squirming away from me, chattering loudly in a language known only to herself. I let her stand up, but then I stuck her ever so slightly with the diaper pin. I should have used the disposable diapers. Bridget had gotten a supply of them before leaving me with her four interesting offspring for a week.

I had spurned the disposable diapers on the grounds that they were not ecologically sound. I was going to be supersitter. I was going to have everything under control. I'd been in charge for a total of two hours, fifteen minutes, and already it was disintegrating all over the place.

Moira stopped screaming about the diaper-pin stick. Really, it was no more than a poke, hardly breaking the skin, but for some reason she didn't like it. She didn't like the way I'd put the big piece of cloth on her, either. When I set her on the floor, she stood up and started pushing the diaper down over her nonexistent hips in a businesslike way.

Bloodthirsty screams came from the backyard. Framed in the window, I saw Corky, the seven-year-old, whack his brother Sam with what looked like a big bone. I blinked, but the weapons didn't change. Sam, five, also armed with a bone, hollered with outrage and swung back. Mick, the three-year-old, dug placidly in the sandbox. While I watched, he used a reddish-brown curve of cranium to scoop up some sand. He picked something out of the sand he'd scooped and regarded it thoughtfully before popping it into his mouth.

I grabbed Moira's small, damp palm and hurried her out of the room. Two hours, twenty minutes, and counting. It was going to be a long week.

How had this happened to me? Liz Sullivan, confirmed spinster, good at ducking commitments. Of course, I felt a sense of obligation to Bridget Montrose, a woman so nice she worries about hurting her occasional cleaning service's feelings by telling them they missed a spot. Bridget and Emery had been looking forward to their Hawaiian vacation for months. Emery was attending a conference, and Bridget was wild to go with him. She'd mentioned several times that she hadn't been away from the kids since before Mick was born. She'd lined up her mother to come from the Midwest and stay with the kids for the week of the conference. She and Emery had spent evenings poring over guidebooks, trying to figure out how to get the most out of their six days.

Then Bridget's mother had broken her ankle. She'd begged off of watching four active children while tottering around on crutches, and I could see why. A person would need to be totally able-bodied. In fact, I felt much too old for the job, and I was only thirty-five.

I went out on the back porch with Moira's little hand clasping mine, the diaper it had taken me several minutes to put on sagging down around her tiny butt. Corky and Sam were still facing off with their femurs. I thought they must be some kind of Flintstone-related toy bones, until I heard the solid thwack they made when the boys engaged again.

"Corky. Sam. Drop your bones."

Sullenly, the boys complied, casting hate-filled glances at each other. Most of the time, Bridget's children were pretty easygoing and had a lot of fun with each other. But Corky and

2

Sam were old enough to realize that their folks weren't coming back for a while.

"He started it," Sam said, pointing at his older brother.

Corky's brilliant red hair blazed in the sun when he tossed his head. "Yeah, well, you asked for it." His sneer couldn't have been bettered by Hollywood coaching.

I picked up Moira to go down the steps, noticing once more that a fourteen-month-old child was not really small when you carried her. She didn't want to be carried. She wanted to do it herself, judging from the way her small fists pummeled my chest. But I had a mission. I went over to the sandbox. Sure enough, Mick was using a piece of skull for his sand-sifting. Sure enough, he was finding little bits of unidentified matter, which I suspected were cat poop, to gnaw on.

"Spit that out, Mick. It's nasty."

He looked up at me, considering. "No," he said. He was a boy of few words.

I hooked a finger through his mouth to get everything out, as I'd seen Bridget do a thousand times. He bit me. At least, the thing he'd been gnawing on was nothing worse than a mummified plum pit from the tree overhanging the sandbox.

I grabbed the piece of skull and put it on the picnic table along with the big bones the boys had been using. The gruesome collection gave me a bad feeling.

"Where did you get these bones?"

Corky and Sam looked at each other and away, united now against the common enemy. I softened my voice. I'm not used to talking much with kids. In the past, treating them as small adults has worked okay. But now that I was the authority figure, it wasn't going over so well.

"Listen, you're not in trouble about the bones. You're in trouble because you broke one of your mom's rules."

"Yeah, yeah. No hitting." Corky looked bored. "We weren't really hitting. We were just—swatting."

3

"He was hitting," Sam insisted stubbornly. "We were playing apes from *2001*, and he started hitting me."

"Where did you find the bones?"

Corky jerked his head toward the front of the house. "You said we could," he said defensively. Sam was more easygoing, but Corky, thin and intense, often had a chip on his shoulder. I swallowed my first impulse, and sat on the picnic table bench, bringing me closer to his level.

"I don't remember what I said you could do."

"You said we could escalate," Sam chimed in.

Corky snorted in disgust. "Excalate, dummy."

"No name-calling." The rules were coming automatically to mind. I have baby-sat for the Montrose kids, but only for the evening. At some point they go to bed. I wished devoutly that instead of being nine A.M., it was nine P.M. "You were excavating? I remember now."

"Yeah, like you said. Where they're tearing up the sidewalk." Corky jerked his head again. "There's lots of bones in there." For the first time, a thought struck him. "Are they real?"

They looked real to me, although they were a mottled brown, not the ivory color I would have expected. I ran a finger down the length of one long bone; it felt gritty. "I don't know."

"I thought," Corky stammered, losing some of his attitude, "I thought they were like dinosaur things. This guy I know, for his birthday party we dug in this pile of dirt in his backyard, and we found dinosaur bone things. His mom put them there."

"She did?" Sam was disappointed. He'd been to the party, too, it seemed. "I thought real dinosaurs lived in Jeffrey's backyard."

"Dummy." The response was automatic. I forgot to correct him, but Sam did it for me with a quick punch to the stomach.

"Am not!"

"That's enough." I picked up the bones and the skull and looked over at the sandbox. "Mick, don't eat anything in there. Let's all go look where the sidewalk was."

4

Every so often in Palo Alto, the city replaces tilting or broken sidewalks, more, I suspect, to avoid liability than to pamper the residents. A magnolia tree in the parking strip before Bridget's house had raised the pavement, and a city crew had come by earlier in the week to tear out the old chunks of sidewalk and pare the roots of the tree, leaving smooth, flat dirt for the next crew, which would pour new concrete there.

The boys had done a good job of excavating, I had to give them that. I had told them they could, soon after Bridget and Emery left for the airport that morning. It was Corky's idea, but the thought of digging had made Sam much more cheerful, as anything involving dirt is likely to do for seven- and five-year-olds. And since Mick and Moira were both howling, I'd only made the condition that they had to put all the dirt back when they finished, and let them go at it.

They'd put the dirt back all right, although the careful mountain they'd built between the stakes and strings was unlikely to endear them to the Public Works crew. Despite its being Saturday, the hard hats were out in force down the street a little way, clanging around with huge metal plates to cover the holes they had dug in the pavement. So far they hadn't noticed the boys' work. All this tearing up is called maintaining the infrastructure, although its most obvious effect is creating a lot of noise and traffic problems.

"See?" Corky pulled a slender, curved, brownish wand out of the dirt pile and brandished it. "There's lots of those bones. Long, skinny ones like cutlasses." He spoke with relish, but then cast a doubtful glance my way. "If they're not play bones, what are they?"

"I don't know." Evidently the sidewalk crew hadn't found any bones when they'd pruned the magnolia roots. "We'd better find out, though. Let's go inside. You boys can fix a snack, while I try to figure out who to talk to."

I kept an eye on the snack-making while I phoned one Public Works number after another. I learned several things, the most important of which is that no one is available on Saturdays. The sidewalks were contracted out to a construction firm, which had the most intricate voice mail I'd ever heard—after several minutes of pressing one and entering pound, I was lost. The city voice mail claimed that in an emergency, someone would get back to me. Considering the state of the bones, I couldn't really say it was an emergency.

Eventually, of course, I called Paul Drake. As soon as a skull came into it, I'd known it would involve him. Paul Drake is a homicide detective for Palo Alto, where Bridget and I both live. He lives here, too; in fact, he lives right in front of my house, a couple of blocks from the scene of the bone find. Of course, since it was Saturday morning, he wouldn't be quite so excited to hear that I wanted him in his professional capacity.

In fact, it appeared to be quite early on Saturday morning from his point of view. His answer to the telephone was a grumpy monosyllable.

Having been up for what seemed like hours—not only up, but engaged in nonstop combat duty—I had no sympathy. "Drake. I need you to come and look at some bones."

"Your bones?" He yawned through the phone. "You want me to jump them?"

This was rather heavy-handed of him, but since he'd obviously not had his morning espresso, I forgave him. "No. These bones are dead. Very dead, from the look of things."

"Human bones? Really?" He sounded more awake.

"I don't know." I looked at the cranium. It wasn't a whole skull—just a bowl-shaped curve about the size of the back of my head. "But could be, I guess."

He yawned again. "Where are you, anyway?" It must have just occurred to him that if I'd found bones at home, I'd be knocking on his back door by now.

"I'm at Bridget's, remember? You're supposed to be taking care of Barker for me while I take care of things here."

"Right." I could hear various rustling noises, and created a

6

picture of Drake in his rumpled bed. Although I have seen Drake in his bed in early morning dishabille, I haven't been in there myself, despite being invited, and despite thinking quite a lot about the invitation.

Drake's not a tall man, or particularly handsome. He's a few years older than I, with wild, curly, graying hair and granny glasses. But his body is surprisingly muscular for someone with his stocky build, and he has a teddy-bear quality that is very appealing when he's caught off-guard, as he would be in the morning.

"Okay," he said, after a moment. "I've got my glasses on. I'll get dressed and bring Barker over. It's probably nothing more than an Indian burial—they're sometimes found near San Francisquito Creek. Don't let the boys stir it up any more than they already have."

He hung up before I could think of a retort to that implied criticism. I sliced the bagels I'd brought with me, wondering if disturbing ancient Indian bones would bring unhappy ancestral spirits down on my head. I don't need extra bad vibes in my life. There are plenty to go around already.

With his mouth full of bagel, Corky harangued me about moving all the dirt again to put the femurs and the rest back with the other bones. "We should put them back," he insisted. "It's the scene of the crime, Aunt Liz."

Sam was not up for this. He was spooked by the idea that they were not fake dinosaur bones. "They're dirty," he said fastidiously, as if this were normally any kind of deterrent to him. "We shouldn't touch them. Right, Aunt Liz?"

The spirited discussion stopped just short of physical violence. Finally I gave Corky permission to arrange the bones he'd already found in a cardboard box in any way he wanted, as long as he stayed on the front porch and didn't bring any specimens inside. Sam drank extra juice and seemed to feel better about it all. At any rate, he announced that "Reading Rainbow" was on and settled in front of the TV.

Corky was back within minutes to join Sam and Mick in front of the TV. I changed Moira again after all that juice. Her eyelids were at half-mast; she'd been up early to say good-bye to Bridget and Emery. I hoped she would have a nice long morning nap, which the schedule Bridget had given me indicated would happen. I rocked her, and gradually she got heavier and heavier until she fell asleep. Putting her to bed, I comforted myself with the thought that although the weekend stretched before me with hours to fill until Monday morning, the children would be going back to school then, even Mick, and I would only have Moira to deal with. I might be able to get a breath or two in then.

Unless the bones turned into something major. I collapsed on the front porch steps, staring at the mountain of dirt the boys had made and wondering what the odds were of them being, after all, dinosaur bones.

2

SITTING there on Bridget's front porch, I took a minute to appreciate the morning coolness. It would be hot by noon. Our ocean breezes often die off in September and October, making them the hottest months in the Bay Area's year. Bridget's one straggly rosebush was blighted with rust and black spot; I started picking the bad leaves off the poor thing into the yellow plastic bucket the boys had left on the porch. The rose had an anemic pink bloom of no particular scent. Before Bridget and Emery returned, I would bring over a bouquet from my own roses, which had also found the summer trying, but were giving me wonderful, fragrant blooms—dark, satiny Oklahoma and Margaret Merrill's sturdy white prettiness.

I heard scrabbling feet on the sidewalk and held on tight to the bucket of dead leaves. A large, galumphing black-and-white dog appeared, towing Paul Drake behind him.

Barker saw me in the yard and launched himself up the sidewalk. You'd think it had been weeks since we'd seen each other instead of just three hours. He'd become a rather well-grown dog in the past four months, with plenty of adolescent energy, and Drake didn't have the hang of walking him at all. And when I say "hang," that's exactly what I mean. Barker didn't take gentle hints about what he should be doing when he was on the leash. Only vigorous jerks on the choke collar conveyed information to him.

Nevertheless, I was glad to see him. And Drake, who looked as rumpled and cuddly as I'd pictured him. He'd had his espresso, though. Otherwise he might not have thought to bring the camera that bounced on his chest while he galloped after the dog.

Drake let go of the leash just before he would have become airborne. "Look, I don't know how you handle this dog. I've got half a foot and probably forty pounds on you, and he didn't slow down all the way here."

"He needs his walk every day." I gave Barker a final pat and made him sit. "You could run him. He loves that."

"I'm busy." Drake had already turned away from me, eyeing the mound of dirt in the former sidewalk area. He whistled. "The boys did all that?"

"With hand tools, no less." I waved the plastic bucket at him. "You want a turn?"

He shook his head. "The fewer people who mess with it at this point, the better."

The words were ominous. I felt a chill on the back of my neck. "You're thinking of it as a crime scene?"

"Not exactly." I knew he was working, then. When Drake starts to hedge, it means he's hoarding information. Anything he drops at that point is on purpose, not by accident. He moved around the pile of dirt, taking pictures. "This is one of the bones?" He zoomed in on the "cutlass" shape the boys had pointed out earlier.

"We've got a box full of them on the porch." I ran up the stairs, closely followed by Barker. He stuck his nose in the cardboard box Corky had filled and quivered all over with doggy eagerness. "Get out of there."

Drake pushed him aside. "Shouldn't have brought this animal," he grumbled. Barker is a bit of a thorn in Drake's side, which made it even nicer of him to agree to oversee my dog while I was preoccupied with Bridget's children. "Are these the ones the boys were playing with?" He cocked his head, listening. "What have you done with them, anyway? It's too peaceful around here."

"Moira's sleeping and the guys are watching TV. Although, if they knew you were here, they'd be all over you." I gave him a sweet smile. "Shall I call them?"

"Please don't. Not yet." He squatted by the box, his attention fixed. He picked up the bones in turn, felt them, held them to his nose, thought about them. I watched him with that strange tightness spreading through my body. Something about Drake when he focused his attention made me wonder what kind of intensity he'd turn on a woman he was involved with. I'd been deflecting that intensity at the critical point for the past few months, but contrarily I wanted to feel it, too, differently from the first time I'd encountered it, when I had been a murder suspect and therefore part of his work.

"So what do you think?" I broke the silence after he'd stared into the treetops across the street for a while.

"Hmm? Oh, I think I'll let this Stanford archaeologist I know take a look first. But—" He shook his head slowly. "The bones have been in the ground for a while. See, they're stained with dirt and they're not waxy anymore, plus there's no trace of gut or sinew."

Speaking of guts, my own twisted. "Great."

"Yeah, makes it harder," he agreed, not exactly getting my point. "But even though they're not particularly fresh, I don't believe they're Costanoan. Indian, you know."

"I know. I've read about Ishi."

"There's more to it than Ishi," he began, then cut himself off. "That's beside the point. I need to use the phone, and then I want to talk to the boys."

The front door opened. "Moira's crying," Corky shouted. He saw Barker and Drake and tumbled out the door, closely followed by Sam and Mick.

Moira was standing in her crib, sobbing. Bridget had told me that she mostly woke up like that, but it was unnerving anyway. She held out her arms to me, then noticed that I wasn't her mom and turned away, increasing the volume.

I patted her back awkwardly, trying to soothe her. My patting hand slipped lower and encountered dampness. Sighing, I hauled Moira out of the crib and over to the changing table. She fixed an apprehensive gaze on my face while I changed her. This time I used a plastic diaper. Even that I couldn't get right; turns out those things have a front and a back. I had to do it a couple of times before it was securely applied.

The menfolk were in the kitchen. Drake listened intently while the boys described their find in shrill, excited voices. I carried Moira on through to the living room, where the TV, abandoned, still blared "Sesame Street." Moira cheered up right away; I sat her on the floor, and she watched intently while Muppets sang and danced about Letter B.

I joined the guys. Corky had talked down Sam and Mick and was finishing the story dramatically. "Then she—" he pointed at me—"said they weren't dinosaur bones. So what are they?"

The three boys watched Drake, their eyes big.

"I'm not sure," he said diplomatically. "I'm going to get an expert to look at them. But it's very important that you boys stay away from the sidewalk now. Okay?"

Their faces fell. "I'll need your help in other ways," Drake finished up lamely. He stood, and they stood too. All of them looked a little downcast.

"How about some cookies?" I felt I should play the traditional role. And Bridget had left a fresh batch of her famous oatmeal-raisin-chocolate chip cookies. It seemed like the right moment to bring them out.

The boys had grape juice with theirs, growing purple mustaches in the process. I made Drake a cup of tea, which he drank because he knew my coffee is hopeless. I keep a jar of instant—a very small jar—for people who feel that they need coffee. I prefer tea, and good tea, too. Bridget had gotten a supply of very expensive Assam; a Post-it note on the little golden bag from the tea store downtown exhorted me to drink up, so I did.

In some telepathic way, the boys decided all at once to play basketball, and ran into the backyard, where their dad had put up a hoop somewhere between Corky's abilities and Mick's. Drake and I stood at the kitchen door, watching them bounce up and down the patio.

"They're good kids," he said, pulling me closer with an arm around my shoulder. I heard a hidden meaning in his words. I have no desire for the domestic-goddess role; the closest I ever come is making muffins out of leftover oatmeal, a skill that doesn't exactly ring the bell on the homemaker scale. Just getting to the point of wanting a man in my bed, after years of keeping them—keeping everyone—at arm's length, was major for me. At the rate I was going, I'd be menopausal before I could commit to a relationship. And that would be fine with me. I sensed it wouldn't be fine with Drake, though. Not only was he stepping up the intimate little touches and kisses, he had made more than one comment that seemed to hint at a desire for children. This was a problem for me. I'm not interested in that scene. And I had tried to let Drake know it.

"They fight a lot, but they don't really hurt each other." I moved away from him, on the pretext of checking Moira, who was still glued to "Sesame Street," watching Big Bird sing a soulful tune about being friends. "Looking after them is very tiring, though. I feel like I've been doing it for weeks instead of just a few hours."

"I'll help," Drake volunteered. Right then and there, I decided that if he thought getting all domestic with me was going to make me want children of my own, he would find out differently. I'm not going to be saddled with motherhood. I feel barely able to take care of myself, let alone a small, helpless person whose years of dependency give a parent lots of chances to totally screw up.

13

"You have bones to deal with," I pointed out. "But if you want to help, fine. Maybe you could take us all out to Burger King for dinner."

Drake winced. He loves his meals.

"We'll see." He checked his watch. "I'd better start calling, see if I can locate some people to take a look at these bones." He shook his head. "I have a bad feeling about them."

"So you think they were put there on purpose." I shivered a little. "When could someone do that? Last time the sidewalk was torn up?"

"That would be the best possibility," he said. "Maybe even longer ago, depending on how deep the sidewalk crew went last time. If the boys hadn't dug him up, he probably wouldn't have been found this time around either."

I hadn't really thought of the bones as a person before, a person who wouldn't have chosen to be interred under a sidewalk. "They were digging with garden trowels and plastic shovels, for heaven's sake. How far down could they have gotten?" I tried to picture the scenario, telling myself to approach it as a story and forget about the person who used to inhabit those bones. "And wouldn't it be hard to dig a hole deep enough to bury someone? After all, there's not a lot of time between the crew tearing up the old pavement and coming back to put on the new. Maybe you'd have a few hours late at night to work. Right out there in the open where any insomniac could see you." I warmed to my theme. "And you'd displace a lot of dirt, too. What would you do with that?"

Drake blew thoughtfully on his tea. "Sometimes it takes days for them to come back. When it rains, for instance." He took another cookie, pointing it at me in an admonishing way. "And if you bought yourself a pair of official-looking coveralls, you could dig as deep a hole as you wanted in broad daylight, and just come back at night to put the body in and fill in with dirt. Or if you lived here, I bet no one would notice you

14

digging out front if you said you were taking soil samples or something. Then tip your body in at night, cover up, and you're done."

It didn't sound very likely to me. "Probably you'll want to talk to the Public Works people, if you can get hold of someone there. I called and got a recording—several recordings."

He grinned. "I know the magic number. I do want to talk to the crew from yesterday, see how deep they went, what they noticed. I can go back home and call, or you can let me use this phone."

"Makes no difference to me." I didn't really mean that, of course. In the past Drake has disliked having me involved in his investigations, although my bad karma had dragged me in anyway. This one looked like something I could totally duck, but I was interested in knowing more about who'd left their bones under the sidewalk enough years ago to remove all traces of the person that had inhabited them.

I busied myself cleaning up the juice glasses and sweeping the floor. Kids make for a lot of debris, and Bridget's kitchen is big enough to be quite a chore to sweep. Drake made several phone calls, but I couldn't always hear what he was saying. I did notice that when he had to leave a message, he left his own phone number, not Bridget's. From that I deduced that he wouldn't be staying long.

I was right. After the last call he turned away from the phone and smiled at me. "It will be a novel experience to have you available by telephone instead of holed up in your house with no modern conveniences."

"Maybe I'm not planning to answer the phone." I actually don't like Mr. Bell's device much, which is why I don't have one. Drake lets me receive messages on his phone, during the times when I'm actively seeking temp work or when I need to talk with the editors who buy my freelance magazine articles.

He just gave me that annoying know-it-all male smile.

15

"You'll answer it," he said, coming to hug me, "because it might be Bridget checking up on her kids, and you wouldn't want to worry her."

He was right. I relaxed into the warm embrace, wishing that I hadn't agreed to be burdened with four young children, wishing that I could let myself go with Drake's flow and forget my anxiety. The physical desire he aroused in me was nearly smothered in anxieties, chief among them the fear of failing again at love and commitment and all that grown-up stuff. Although it wouldn't be as physically catastrophic as my marriage had been, to try and then fail with Drake would certainly be devastating.

"Okay," I said, pulling away finally. "I'll answer the phone. But you'll have to let me hang around when the archaeologist comes."

He pushed his granny glasses up. "You have a deal."

3

DRAKE left, mumbling about meeting someone from Public Works. He didn't take Barker with him. Boys and dog tangled in the backyard, along with several tennis balls and a large stick.

I put away the dishes and tried not to feel outnumbered. At least I knew Drake would be back—after all, I had custody of the bones. Still, it seemed hard to be left with four children, all stirred up by dirt and sugar. Even Moira tired of "Sesame Street" and lurched into the kitchen. I smiled at her, and she smiled back before she realized her mother wasn't there. Tears welled up in her big blue eyes.

I picked her up and tried to comfort her. She twisted her little body away from me and increased the volume. To distract her, I pulled a glossy eggplant from the basket of fruit and veggies on the counter and waved it. She cried harder. I tried a crookneck squash and a pear with no success. Finally she accepted a banana, hiccuping out little leftover sobs while she examined it.

"Do you want me to peel it?" I broke the banana stem and started to pull off the skin. It wasn't a good idea. Moira howled, a primitive, heartbroken sound that shook me. I handed the banana back, but she threw it on the floor. Her nose began to run. I realized her hands were dirty when she used them to wipe her eyes and left smears on her flushed cheeks.

Before I could get a washcloth, the doorbell rang. I picked

up the banana with my free hand and carried the howling baby over to the door.

An attractive young woman stood on the porch, her shoulder-length, sun-streaked hair blowing in the breeze. She wore khaki slacks and a plaid shirt with the sleeves rolled up on slender, tanned arms. She pulled her attention away from the cardboard box that held the bones long enough to look at me and my noisy comrade.

"Are you—" she pulled a little notebook out of her leather knapsack and looked at it—"Liz Sullivan?"

"Yes," I said. Moira reached steam-whistle decibels, then stopped abruptly to gaze at the woman.

"I'm Dinah Blakely." She held out her hand. I reached automatically to shake it, forgetting for a moment that I held a partially-peeled, dirt-encrusted banana. Her wide, white smile faded; she dropped her hand. "Paul Drake sent me, Mrs. Sullivan. He said you'd found some interesting bones, and I see he was right." Her gaze strayed back to the box.

I gave Moira the banana, which she clasped while still staring at Dinah Blakely. "The boys found them, actually. And I'm not a Mrs. Just Liz is fine."

Dinah glanced from me to Moira. "Boys? You have—more children?"

"I don't have any children." I pulled a tissue out of my pocket and wiped Moira's nose. She howled again, briefly. "I'm house-sitting and child-sitting. The boys are in the back. Shall I get them?"

Dinah cocked her head. The boys were audible, now that Moira had fallen silent. Their shouts, and Barker's shrill namesake noises, wafted out of the backyard. "That's okay," she said hastily. "I'll just wait here for Paul. He said he'd meet me."

"Feel free to look over the bones," I offered. Moira struggled a little, and I put her down. She made a beeline for Dinah Blakely.

"What a darling little girl," Dinah cooed apprehensively. Moira was very cute, with her feathery red curls and rosy cheeks. But Dinah was looking at her hands, aimed right at the perfectly creased twill trousers.

"Amazing how dirty kids get, isn't it?" I swooped Moira up just before she touched the trousers. "Of course, I guess you know about dirt—you're an archaeologist, right?"

"Anthropologist, actually." Dinah crossed over to the box and squatted beside it, picking up the piece of cranium. "Yes, I've gotten dirty before." Her voice sounded absent. She turned the piece of bone over in her hands. "That's why we wear khaki, you know. It's not just some Indiana Jones thing."

Moira reached for the cranium, and Dinah held it away. "Mustn't touch," she said in the fake voice that childless people keep for children. Talking to kids is hard when you don't have any of your own. I assumed she didn't have any. There was no ring on her finger, either.

"How long have you been doing this?" I gestured to the bones, but it was a minute before Dinah answered. She put down the piece of cranium and picked up one of the long bones.

"Hmm? Oh, for a few years. I've just been at Stanford for about nine months, though. Paul and I met when someone else found bones in the creek bed. But those were from a dog."

Her words sent a chill down my back. "And these aren't?"

"Oh, no." She waved the leg bone at me. "Definitely human."

Drake's rusty Saab pulled into the driveway, and Dinah smiled. "There's Paul." She waved again with the leg bone, this time at Drake. He smiled and waved in return.

"So you beat me, Dinah." He bounded up the steps, pausing to pinch Moira's grubby cheek. "Hello, cutie." He winked at me, and I wasn't certain who the salutation was aimed at. Probably Moira—she's much cuter than I. I am short and nondescript-looking, the kind of woman you see everywhere.

Dinah tossed back her blond hair and rose easily from her

crouching position, earning my respect. It's not that I'm old and creaky. I'm only thirty-five. But my knees seem to be aging ahead of the rest of me.

"Hi, Paul." She gave Drake a big smile, and he responded in kind. "These bones are something."

"Dinah." He shook her hand briskly, the hand that wasn't holding a bone, and gestured at me. "They're Liz's bones, really."

"Bridget's." I spoke firmly, not wanting to claim the bones in any way.

"So what do we have?" Drake bent over the box with Dinah beside him.

"Human. Probably male, though I can't say for certain at this point. But the length of the leg bones and this piece of pelvis here indicate a man. Probably in his twenties, early thirties." She pointed to the end of the leg bone. "See, the growth plates are completely fused, but there are no signs of age-related wear." She looked more closely. "Actually, he might have had a bum knee. See?" She pointed to some minuscule bump on the end of the bone, and Drake nodded wisely.

"Boy, you can tell a lot just from the bones, huh?" I came closer. Moira was eating the banana now, smearing that into the existing matrix of her face. I should have taken her in for a bath, or at least a face wash, but couldn't pull myself away.

Dinah smiled. "Oh, yes. The bones can speak, if you can hear them. If I had a bit of jawbone, now—" She rummaged for a minute in the box and came up empty-handed. "That's the way to make a firm identification. Dental records, you know, although—see?" She picked up a flat, dished piece of bone and examined it. "These have been in the ground for a while. You've got some rodent chew here. Probably gopher or something like that. If you're involved, Paul, maybe it's not rodent chew but sharp-force trauma." She cast a flirtatious smile at Drake.

He smiled back, but I couldn't tell if he was aware of

Dinah's skittish little invitation. At any rate, she turned back to the bones.

"This piece of pelvis is good for telling us stuff. You can see the broad articulation here where it connects to the spine. And no lipping—that indicates a person probably in their early-or mid-twenties." She brought the fragment to her nose and sniffed thoroughly. "And the smell. That candle-wax smell is faint. I'd guess ten, twelve or more years in the ground." She frowned. "That could make an ID harder, even if we find the jawbone. Dentists don't always keep their records that long."

Drake was fascinated. I was, too, reluctantly. Despite Dinah's wholesome appearance, I didn't like the way she looked at Drake. She would give him strong, healthy children who would only be dirty at the proper times. She would help him in his work. She would be better for him than I would, mass of insecurities that I was. If I were a good person, I would quietly fade back into the house and mind my own business while they got on with it.

Not being particularly good, I hung around while Moira scraped the inside of the banana skin with her pearly little teeth. We followed Drake and Dinah down to the sidewalk, listening to their discussion of the best way to deal with the mess the boys had made. Dinah wanted to bring over an archaeology lab class and let them gain experience. Drake wanted to bring in the crime scene team and haul everything away for exhaustive analysis.

Their argument was spirited, between colleagues. I got the banana peel away from Moira and buried it around the dripline of the ratty-looking rosebush, having read in a gardening book that banana peels are good for roses. I made Moira a hollyhock doll to take its place.

"Now, Paul," Dinah said, putting one hand on his arm. "This is an ideal situation. And you don't know it's a crime scene, after all."

"Unless those bones are really old," he said, shaking his

head, "unless they're Ohlone or something, they don't belong under a sidewalk. Only foul play would have put them there."

Dinah chewed her lip. "They're not Costanoan," she said at last, reluctantly. "I could tell by the shape of the skull fragment. Native American skulls have a ridge—" She drew an imaginary line that bisected her own head, as if she were going to put that shiny hair into pigtails.

"And if you had to pin it down, would you say between ten and twenty years, or less?" Drake was intent, leaning toward her.

She sighed. "I'd be inclined to say more than ten, less than twenty, although it's hard to be so precise with bone that's been in the ground for a while." She put her hand on his arm again, leaning forward persuasively. "It's such a great opportunity for our students. We'll dig up everything according to correct excavation technique. We'll find every last piece of anything that's in there—buttons, cloth fragments, you name it. And we'll be able to tell you exactly where in the area under study the fragments came from."

Drake shrugged. "After the Montrose boys stirred everything up, that doesn't matter so much."

Dinah pressed his arm. "So if it's already disturbed, what difference would it make for us to go at it?"

"I'll think about it," Drake said, smiling at her, but disengaging his arm. I could have told her that was as good as saying no, but I didn't.

He came over to me. "This is dull for you, Liz."

"No, I'm riveted."

"Moira's not." Moira was twisting a bit in my grip, but I wouldn't set her down so close to the street. "Listen, I'm getting a crew out here. We're going to tarp the area and put caution tape around it. I've let Public Works know that the sidewalk crews will have to give this one a miss for the time being. So you don't have to worry about it anymore." He squeezed my shoulder. "You look beat. Why don't you go have a cup of tea or something?"

I didn't feel that beat, but probably next to Dinah's dewy youthfulness I did look bad. I took myself off, since that was what he wanted, but I didn't clean Moira up right away. Instead I stood just behind the lace curtain over the front door window and watched while Drake and Dinah conferred. Finally they both drove away in their separate cars, and I went to find a washcloth.

4

THE washcloth made Moira mad. That's why I didn't hear Claudia Kaplan knocking at the door. She was in the living room when I came back.

"Hi, Liz. Hi, sweetie." She came and took Moira out of my arms, and, contrary creature that she was, the baby beamed at her. Of course, Claudia was very comfortable-looking. Her gray hair was pulled back into a rather untidy braid, and her tall, queenly body was encased in one of her many brilliant muumuus. "I saw Drake drive away," she continued, after suitably greeting Moira. "And some woman—young woman." She said the word "young" with a slight emphasis, and looked a question at me. "What's with those butcher's rejects on the front porch? They for Barker?"

I gestured her into the kitchen. "Come in here and have some tea while I check on the boys. It's a long story."

Claudia loved the story; I knew she would. She wrote well-researched biographies of women she considered important; though scholarly enough to gain her the respect of her colleagues, they were also popular enough to provide her with a living, something the rest of us writers envied. I thought of my notes for the article I was writing for *Organic Gardening*. A week hadn't seemed so long to wait before starting it; in fact, I had kind of thought I could just whip it out on Bridget's computer in my spare time. Now I got a glimmering of how difficult that would be with four children around my neck. I wondered how Bridget had ever managed to produce anything, let alone her first novel, which would be published in two months.

"You get all the luck," Claudia said with envy. "Now you'll be able to hear everything about the investigation. I bet this time Drake keeps you filled in."

"It's not my idea of a good time." I poured some more iced tea into Claudia's glass and hit myself again, too. Stimulation would definitely be needed if I were to survive the week. "It's hard enough to ride herd on all these kids without having to deal with the police and all."

"And that young woman. What's her role here?"

"She's the anthropologist."

"Oh." Claudia drank thoughtfully. "She and Drake seemed very . . . friendly."

"They met on a previous investigation. Dog bones, as it turns out."

"And these are truly human?"

"That's right." I watched Moira play with the many strands of Claudia's necklace. Why couldn't she cuddle up to me like that? Admittedly I didn't have Claudia's advantage in the lap department, but it still didn't seem fair.

"Well, how long have they been buried? That seems to me to be the question." Claudia frowned. "You know, I've lived in my same house for nearly thirty years, and I don't remember anything like this happening. Of course—" she waved an inclusive arm—"it would be more likely to happen around here than in my neighborhood. It's more respectable now, but all this used to be rental housing. Students, mostly. In fact, this place was a student rental until Emery and Bridget bought it ten or twelve years ago." She fell silent, her lips moving a bit. "Twelve years," she decided.

"Dinah Blakely, the anthropologist, guessed between ten and twenty years for the bones. But she doesn't really know how long, I think."

Claudia suddenly looked very fierce. "Drake doesn't believe this has anything to do with Bridget or Emery, does he?"

"At times like this, I know very little of what Drake is thinking." I grinned at her. "But I doubt he suspects Bridget of knocking someone off and sticking them under the pavement. How is it that you remember so much about this neighborhood before Bridget and Emery? Your house is in Professorville."

Moira paused in her necklace play and assumed an expression of great concentration. Claudia patted her absently.

"One of Alfred's graduate students lived here for a while," she said. "Let's see, Jack was in elementary school—I think Carlie was, too. During the summer, before all the summer kids' programs were available. This graduate student used to baby-sit for us, until we found out she was taking the children over to her place—" Claudia looked around—"here, and smoking dope with her friends while the kids watched TV." She shook her head. "Real mangy group lived here then. Hippies, drug dealers, you name it. A lot of houses in this area were rented out to groups. Wild parties, loud music. Really, it was everywhere, even down the street from us. Alfred didn't like it. He wanted to move to Crescent Park before Carlie started school, but the prices had gone up, and he decided we couldn't afford to move. And I felt it gave the neighborhood vitality, even if you didn't trust any of those young people as baby-sitters."

Claudia's house, though she didn't keep it in very good repair, would be worth probably twenty times what they'd paid thirty years ago. Even my tumbledown little shack was worth a lot of money. I'd often thought of selling it and moving somewhere cheap. It's just that nowhere seems particularly cheap anymore.

"Do you remember anything about someone who disappeared and was never found?"

Claudia wrinkled her forehead and then, when it delighted Moira, made more faces. "Not really," she said finally. "I wasn't real involved in community things then. Just coping with kids and trying to do some research." She sniffed, and sniffed again. "Speaking of coping—"

"I figured as much." I stood up. "I'll change her."

"Let me," Claudia suggested, heaving herself to her feet while holding Moira a little away. "I haven't changed a diaper in a long time."

"I won't fight you for it." I went to the back door and watched for a minute while the boys threw tennis balls for Barker, and he played keep-away with them, a game he much preferred to fetch. Then he started teaching them to fetch; after they threw the ball, he stood there, his head cocked, and they eventually ran to get it. It was as good a way as any I could have devised to tire them out. I left them to it.

Claudia came back, holding Moira's hand while she toddled tippily along. "I still know how to put a diaper on," she bragged. "Such knowledge is never really lost. Maybe I'm ready to be a grandmother now, if my kids would only cooperate."

She'd used a cloth diaper, and it was snug, not drooping anywhere. "That's great," I said. "Can you show me?"

She spent a few minutes showing me how to fold and pin a diaper. Then the boys came in, bursting with high spirits and followed by an excited Barker.

They were glad to see Claudia, who must have seemed like an ocean liner of familiarity in a cast-adrift world, and showered her with fervent hugs.

"'Say, I know." She gathered the boys into a huddle. "How about I take you fellows down to the Peninsula Creamery for a milkshake?"

We were all enthusiastic about that. I just had one reservation. "Uh, Claudia—you will be walking, right? Not driving?"

"If you insist," she said huffily. Claudia's driving was famous for its wretchedness. Considering her plunging, absent-minded method of progression, her actual lack of

27

accidents was thought by her friends to be positive proof for the concept of guardian angels. However, I didn't want to risk that this expedition would be the time that Claudia had the accident she'd deserved for years.

I watched them down the street, Claudia puffing along pushing Mick in the stroller while Corky and Sam ranged ahead. Moira wept a little in a desultory way, but was placated by sitting in the high chair with Cheerios and apple slices on the tray. For a few minutes she ate happily while I swept a fresh accumulation of dirt off the faded linoleum, which was not much newer than my own ancient floor covering.

Bridget and Emery hadn't remodeled their early-1900s bungalow, although she was always talking about doing it. Except for a newish refrigerator, the kitchen probably looked much as it had for the past fifty years, roughly the age of the Wedgewood stove. The cabinets and woodwork were from the same era as those in my place, a time when cabinets were made from solid wood, painted with thick white enamel, and placed scantily around wainscoting-clad walls. It was charming, if run-down, and at least Bridget had a walk-in pantry for actual storage. Despite its age and inconvenience, her kitchen was homey and welcoming.

Bridget had mentioned once that she and Emery had painted over a lot of Day-Glo colors before they moved in. I could imagine the marijuana brownie–baking sisters from the seventies in the kitchen, along with their long-haired, draft-dodger boyfriends, before cynicism and life brushed the bloom off them, listening to Hendrix and toking up. My sister, eight years older, had worn platform shoes and skirts as short as she could get away with; the arguments about her skirt length had made an impression on an eight-year-old. By the time I was old enough to rebel, the initial parental shock over bell bottoms and torn jeans had dissipated; impassioned discussion of the principles of peace and love had given way to uninterested acceptance of bizarre dress and provocative pronouncements.

I still held those times up in my mind as purer, less sullied than the era of greed that followed. However, my feelings probably had more to do with my own wide-eyed youth than with historical truth. And it's been a long time since abstract virtues have had any impact on my life.

Moira contributed some Cheerios and an apple slice to the dirt I was sweeping, so I took her down from the high chair, washing her face again. We settled in the living room with a basket of bristle blocks. It was nearly lunchtime; I wondered if the boys would still be hungry after milkshakes. I also wondered if Claudia would survive. I should have taken Moira in the stroller and gone with her, but the notion of having just one child to tend for a while had been too enticing. I stuck some bristle blocks together to form a frame and prayed to survive the week.

Barker roused from the blissed-out sleep of a well-exercised dog and began living up to his name. Startled, Moira turned a worried face to me. I picked her up and went to the door, expecting the mail carrier.

A battered white van with the Stanford emblem on the side panel had pulled up in the driveway. Several people were milling around, directed by a tall, slim man whose long, graying hair was pulled back in a ponytail.

Moira and I went out on the porch. I let Barker out, too, but I kept a hand in his collar.

"Excuse me," I said politely. "What are you doing?"

No one paid any attention. Besides the ponytailed man in charge, three other jeans-clad people hauled shovels and other equipment out of the van. All of them wore baseball caps. One was a woman in her early twenties, I judged. The other two were men about the same age.

I raised my voice. "Hey!"

The older man looked at me and held up his hand in a laconic wave. Barker began growling. He doesn't like men much until he gets to know them. Sometimes not then.

"Hey! What are you doing!"

The older man came over, stopping at the front of the porch steps when he heard Barker's growl. His three companions quit working and watched.

"Hi. You the home owner?" The ponytailed man smiled. His face was lean, with leathery skin and pale, almost silvery blue eyes. The charming smile revealed a flash of gold tooth back among his molars. His sleeveless T-shirt emphasized a limber, attractively muscled build, showing a bit of curling grayish chest hair. A red bandanna was tied jauntily around his neck.

"I'm living here. Who are you?"

His grin widened. "You get to the point, don't you. Will your dog bite?"

"Probably." I kept my finger in Barker's collar. He still had his fur raised, though it wouldn't take much friendliness from the man to make Barker his buddy for life. He's a good watchdog for five minutes, then he wants to play.

The man laughed, gold tooth flashing. "Well, I hope he doesn't. I'm Richard Grolen, from the archaeology department. At Stanford," he added when I frowned.

"That's nice. Why are you here?"

He shook his head, still smiling. "Man. I guess Dinah didn't tell you. We're the excavation team." He jerked a thumb over his shoulder, indicating the group of students who leaned against the van.

"Dinah told you to come?"

He settled his thumbs in the belt loops of his worn jeans. They fit him, I noticed, very well. "She said you had some bones to dig up." He looked at the pile of dirt where the sidewalk used to be. One of the rib bones still stuck out. "I see what she means. This will be great lab work."

He moved as if to turn away. I tightened my grip on Barker's collar, and he growled again. "Did she also tell you," I said, "that the police don't want you to dig them up?"

30

"They don't?" Richard Grolen's face registered shocked surprise. "No, she didn't mention that. Truth to tell, I haven't actually spoken with her. She left a message with this address, said she was looking into it as a lab site."

"She looked. It isn't."

He took off his baseball cap and brushed one hand over the top of his head, where the straight, gray-blond hair was thinning. "Thing is," he said confidentially, "we were heading for a site up near Jasper Ridge and we got kicked out. There's a big butterfly count going on or something, and they were afraid we'd disturb the bugs." He smiled disarmingly. "So when I got her message we were already loaded up looking for a place to dig. So . . ." He shrugged, moving those nice chest muscles in an interesting way. "Here we are. Rarin' to go."

Moira started squirming to get down. Barker pulled at his collar. One of the students called plaintively, "Should we get the stakes out, Dr. Grolen?"

A doctor, yet. "Look," I said, starting to lose my grip on child, dog, and temper. "The police want to do their own investigation here. You'll have to talk to them before you can lift so much as one shovelful of dirt."

Richard Grolen frowned. His voice was a little crisper. "You know, the sidewalk isn't on your property or anything. I'll take care of the police. You don't have to worry about this at all."

"That's what you think." I knew how Drake would feel about the archaeology department moving in on his bones, no matter how charming their representatives. "I can't control the dog anymore."

Luckily a bigger force of nature was unleashed, before Barker could bound down the stairs and kill the students with big, wet, dog kisses. Melanie Dixon's BMW drew up to the curb. She climbed out, tightening her mouth in disapproval when she saw the pile of dirt. She scanned and dismissed the students before lighting on Richard Grolen at the foot of the stairs. Her eyes widened.

"Why, Richard!" She hurried up the sidewalk and took his hands, laughing. "Richard Grolen! How nice to see you again, after all this time!"

Richard's face wore that charming smile again. "Melanie! Good God, this takes me back. As if this neighborhood wasn't enough, now you're here!"

"It's been so long." She gave him a dainty hug and stepped back. "You look just the same, you old pirate. What have you been up to? Why are you at Bridget's house?"

Richard gave me the tail end of the smile. "Is this Bridget? You're Melanie's friend? Small world, isn't it?"

"Don't be silly." Melanie scowled at me as if I had been guilty of impersonation. "This is Liz. What in the world is happening here, Liz? What's that?" A toss of her head, which hardly disturbed her shiny, perfectly cut brown hair, indicated the dirt pile. "Why are you keeping Richard standing in the yard?"

"I'm not keeping him at all. He can leave now." Melanie and Bridget are both part of a poet's group that meets regularly in Palo Alto, and they both have young children. Aside from those points in common, they are an ill-assorted pair to be friends. Bridget has a warmth and common sense valued by everyone she knows; Melanie comes from a well-connected Palo Alto family and knows something, usually something detrimental, about everyone who's anyone in this town. She is not much taller than I am, always perfectly groomed, and always seems skeptical of my right to live in the same town that she does.

Richard took Melanie aside for a low-voiced conversation. I told Barker to sit, and for a wonder he did. I gave Moira the bristle blocks I still had in my hand, and she amused herself by throwing them at Richard.

A dull roar came from somewhere down the street, growing louder and louder. The students craned their necks, peering down the sidewalk. Even Richard broke off to listen.

Claudia and the three boys lurched into view. They might have been drunks coming home from a carouse, especially since they were singing, at the top of their lungs, "Ninety-nine bottles of beer on the wall." Actually, they had reached eighty-three. Claudia sang, too, providing a bass note.

Melanie sighed in disgust. Claudia and the boys, pausing in front of the driveway for a grand finale, attempted some harmony. "Eighty-two bottles of beer on the wall," they howled happily.

"Really, Claudia." Melanie spoke as soon as she could make herself heard.

The boys flung themselves at the steps to hug Barker, and he writhed happily. "We had beer!" Corky shrieked. "Lots of beer!"

"Root beer," Claudia amended. "Hello, Melanie. Who's this?" She gave Richard Grolen an interested stare.

Before Melanie could reply, Drake's car pulled up and he charged up the front walk. He had noticed the Stanford van, and he didn't look happy.

I sat down on the porch step, deafened by the kids' screams and Barker's answering yowls. Moira took careful aim and hurled the last of the bristle blocks, bouncing it with great accuracy off the center of Drake's forehead.

It was going to be a long afternoon.

5

DESPITE those intoxicating root beer floats, the boys demanded lunch. I was happy to slink away from the melee in the front yard. Melanie had assumed hostess duties and was introducing a glowering Drake to Richard Grolen, while Claudia gave Richard the frank, approving once-over she reserves for sexy younger (to her, anyway) men.

Moira and I ushered the boys into the house. I checked the list of acceptable food items Bridget had posted on the refrigerator, and got out the peanut butter. In just seven hours they would all go to bed ("Eight P.M. firm for bedtime," Bridget had written. "Seven-thirty for Mick if he's getting cranky.") and I would be free to collapse.

Corky helped himself to juice and splashed it on the floor. Sam protested the waste and got his own mug out. I took control of the juice pitcher but lost the peanut butter knife to Mick, who pushed a chair up to the counter and loaded the knife up before looking around for a target. The front door opened, and Barker took the role of doorbell.

I finished pouring juice and regained control of the peanut butter knife. Melanie Dixon appeared at the kitchen door.

"Do you think we could get some tea or coffee or something?" Melanie's hair was mussed and her eye makeup smudged. Given her usual impeccable appearance, this was a sure sign that something had her ruffled.

Claudia pushed through the kitchen door after her. "Don't

be silly, Melanie." She plucked Mick off the chair he was tee-
tering on and set him firmly in his booster seat at the table.
"Can't you see Liz has her hands full? I notice you're not burdened with your children this morning."

"I left them with Maria," Melanie said stiffly. Her glance at
the Montrose quartet spoke volumes; her perfect little daughters, Amanda and Susana, would never be so vociferous. "I just
stopped by on my way home from the farmers' market, to
make sure things were going all right with Biddy's kids."

When I went to the farmers' market, which I rarely did
unless I was selling my own produce, I generally ended up
with little bits of the free samples stuck about my person—a
dab of plum pulp, some nectarine juice, a couple of dribbled
tomato seeds. Melanie, of course, had escaped that. The con-
trast seemed even greater to me because our hair is much the
same color brown and we're about the same height, although
she is definitely thinner. She has a thick, turned-under,
shoulder-length bob; my hair is short, since I hack it off when
it gets in my way.

When she glanced around the kitchen, I immediately felt
like a feebleminded failure. Moira, banging on the high-chair
tray, had created a new floor design of small circles and half
circles, using the rest of her Cheerios and apple slices. Mick
picked up one of the apple slices and offered it to Barker, who
licked it and then backed away. Mick promptly began to chew
on the slice. Sam had spilled his juice down the front of his
already dirty T-shirt, and was loudly demanding more. Corky
grabbed a banana and dropped the rest of the bunch on the
floor.

I took the half-eaten slice of apple away from Mick and
raised my voice over the resultant protest. "It's going fine,
thanks, Melanie."

She raised one perfectly shaped eyebrow. "I see."

"Chaotic, though." I finished spreading peanut butter on
bread and cut the one sandwich into four pieces, hoping to fill

four mouths to the point of silence with it. Corky grabbed the knife and began spreading peanut butter onto his banana. The banana peel reposed elegantly on his head, which made Sam shriek with laughter.

"Yes, isn't it?" Melanie inspected a chair and sat down. I found myself hoping that she'd overlooked something dark and squishy, which she wouldn't know was on the back of her slacks until she'd been in every store on University Avenue.

Claudia filled the teakettle with water. "I'll make some coffee," she volunteered. "I know Bridget has some instant somewhere in here."

Melanie and I exchanged glances. I don't drink coffee, but Drake did, and I'd watched him make it often enough to know that only the best beans, freshly ground, went into his brew.

Melanie got up with reluctance. "I'll make the coffee." She looked through the door into the living room as she passed.

"How are the negotiations coming?" Claudia lounged against the counter, arms folded across her ample bosom.

Melanie rummaged in a cupboard and came away with a box of coffee filters. She found the pot, then looked in the freezer. "Ah!" She held up a bag of coffee. "What negotiations?"

"Isn't that why Drake kicked us both out? So he and that hunky archaeologist could dicker?" Claudia grinned at Melanie. "Were the two of you involved in the past? You seemed very friendly."

"I'm not at all friendly with Detective Drake." Melanie's lips thinned while she measured coffee. "I find him boorish and sly."

This tickled Claudia. "No, no," she chortled. "Not Drake. The archaeologist. What's his name?"

"Oh, Richard." Melanie loosened up a little. "I knew him years ago when we were both students. Of course," she remembered to add, "he was much older than me. An upperclassman, and he'd done his military service, too." A reminiscent smile quirked her lips.

"So was this during your wild period?" Claudia looked interested. She was incredibly nosy, like any good biographer; even if she weren't really interested in the story of your life, she would probe for details as long as there was an opening.

Melanie, however, wasn't open. "None of your business," she snapped. "I don't know what you're talking about."

Claudia didn't say any more, but now my curiosity was aroused. I didn't really care if Melanie had been wild in her youth or not. But since the gory details of my past had been displayed rather spectacularly over the past year or so, especially among the group of writers that hung out together, I didn't see why Melanie should have immunity. And since she'd grown up in Palo Alto, I was sure I could find out whatever I wanted to know. Then, next time she looked down her nose at me, I would find comfort in knowing she, too, was only human. Call me petty, but there it is.

I cut another peanut butter sandwich into fourths. This time I got fancy and cut off the crusts, which no one was eating anyway. Corky left half of his peanut-butter banana on the table. Sam was wearing the peel now. Mick ate steadily through the sandwiches. Moira knuckled her eyes, leaving a smear of peanut butter on her cheek.

The water boiled, and Melanie poured it into the coffee filter. Drake pushed the kitchen door open, sniffing.

"Is there coffee?" He gave Melanie a smile, but she tossed her head. She did smile for Richard Grolen, though, who followed Drake through the door and stopped.

"Unbelievable." He looked around the kitchen. "It looks just the same. Well, maybe not just the same—new refrigerator, different furniture."

Drake gave him a look. "You used to live here, Mr. Grolen?"

Richard Grolen pulled his head out of the pantry. "Different paint, too. The wainscoting used to be yellow and purple stripes." He looked at Drake. "No, we—I lived across the street. But I was over here a good deal. Real tight group of people lived on this block, man. You know, Melanie."

Melanie squirmed a little. "Well, I was very busy then, Richard."

He started to argue. "You lived here for how long? A year?"

"Richard—"

He noticed her discomfort. "Right. We had some good times, though."

"Bit of a coincidence," Drake said. His voice was casual, but his eyes were intent. "That you were the one who came to try and haul my bones away."

Richard held up his hands. "Now, wait a minute. I haven't ceded you custody of those bones by any means."

Drake regarded him in an unfriendly fashion. "Look, Grolen. This is not an archaeological site. Pack your shovels and find somewhere else to dig."

"Now, Detective—" Richard Grolen gave Drake a charming smile.

Drake didn't smile back. "According to your own colleague, Ms. Blakely, the bones are very unlikely to be Costanoan or to have any historical significance, Dr. Grolen. What has significance for us is that they appear to have been deliberately placed under the sidewalk, which would limit them to the twentieth century—hardly interesting to archaeologists."

Richard Grolen raised an eyebrow. "Not at all. Since we do less digging of ancient ruins now than we used to—"

"Less?" Claudia interrupted. "Why do you do less digging? Are there fewer ancient sites?"

"We find new sites constantly," Richard told her, warming to her interest. "But we know now that our methods of excavating are crude compared with techniques that will be used in the future. So our approach now is to preserve the sites until technology allows us to excavate without destroying what we're trying to understand."

Drake had been fidgeting during this. "At any rate, we don't want to preserve this site. We just want to get to the bottom of it."

Melanie giggled, and the rest of us smiled. "Why don't you just let Richard's group dig it up?" she said. "You're going to dig it up anyway, right? It'll save city resources to let him."

"That's right," Richard chimed in eagerly. I spared a thought for those students, presumably left outside while the grownups consulted.

"I don't want to wait weeks for you to finish, and I don't think Bridget would either," Drake pointed out. "I want that body out of there and evaluated by the coroner's office so we can determine what we have."

"That's going to be difficult if you just haul the bones out," Richard said, inspecting his fingernails. "For instance, if there was a bullet in the chest cavity, you have to excavate down through the cavity to find it. What good is it as evidence if it's just sifted out of a pile of rubble?"

"If a bullet is found in the vicinity of the body, it makes a pretty obvious statement," Drake said, but he looked undecided.

Melanie said thoughtfully, "That's true about Biddy, though. She shouldn't have to put up with weeks of digging going on, not with everything else."

"Who's this Biddy?" Richard Grolen asked, irritated.

"Bridget," Claudia corrected. "She's in Hawaii."

"Well, then." Figuratively, Richard washed his hands.

"She'll be back Friday," Melanie said. "Can you complete a dig in that length of time, Richard?"

Now Richard chewed his lip, thinking. Drake said nothing.

"Not ordinarily," he said at last. "But as you pointed out, Detective, this isn't a site with historical importance. If we just wanted to work on our excavating skills, guess we could hurry it up. After all, the bones aren't in there very deep."

Melanie turned to Drake, triumphant. "See! I've saved you some money."

"Not really, Mrs. Dixon." Drake kept his voice polite, but I could tell he found Melanie irritating. He wasn't the only one. "We'll still have to have someone here the whole time, making sure nothing gets—mislaid." He darted a look at Richard. "Especially if it turns out to be a homicide. After all, your friend here might have had an opportunity to plant someone under the sidewalk while he was living across the street. It wouldn't look good for us to give him access to his own crime scene, now would it?"

Melanie sputtered with indignation, but Richard threw back his head and laughed. "Right," he said. "I might make away with the evidence. That would never do."

"I'm not making a decision right now," Drake said firmly. "In any case, it's not just my decision to make. After I talk to a few people, I'll let you know."

Richard handed Drake a card. "Guess that's the best I'm going to do," he said, resigned. "I'll haul my people out of here. But we'll be ready to come back whenever you say so."

Melanie escorted Richard out. Claudia watched them go, then looked at Drake. "You know," she said conversationally, "Melanie knows a lot about what was going on around here fifteen, twenty years ago. She was the one who steered Biddy to this house when it went up for sale, after the old lady who owned it passed away. You should try to get on her good side, Drake."

"I don't have to get on anyone's good side." The whole encounter had evidently rubbed Drake the wrong way. He looked around the kitchen, at the munching kids and slumbering dog, at Claudia's amused face and at me. I tried to arrange an expression of sympathetic interest, but didn't know how much good it did.

40

Drake gulped down the coffee Claudia handed him, and glared at me. "Keep those kids away from that dirt," he ordered. "The Public Works guys should be here soon to secure the site. I'll be at home if you need me, trying to get my weekend back."

He stalked out.

Claudia looked at me with sympathy. "Listen," she said, setting her own coffee cup down. "Don't try to be a hero here. Bridget left some housekeeping money, right?" I nodded. "Take the kids out for pizza if you have to, but take it easy on yourself. You've got several days to go—don't wear out now."

It was good advice. I cut up more apple, and some pear for variety, and decided that we would all have enforced quiet time after lunch.

I, especially, needed it.

6

THE kids went down for well-deserved naps. Stillness blessed the house.

Sinking into one of the shabby overstuffed chairs in the living room, I took the *Utne Reader* from the pile of magazines on the coffee table. Afternoon sun from the window at my back threw warmth and light over my shoulder. The rapid decline of the ozone layer, and the writer's concern about it, began to blur in front of my eyes. I drifted off.

I woke suddenly when a racket started outside. Disoriented, I sprang from the chair, dumping the *Utne Reader* on the floor. Barker, dozing at my feet, also jumped up and started to contribute to the noise before I could shush him.

I peeped in the door to the boys' room. Mick lay snuggled with his blanket. Corky, with *Tintin in America* open beside him, stirred in his sleep. Sam's head was pillowed on another Tintin book. He snored a little.

I closed the door to their room, and to Moira's. Barker followed me, his fur raised, low growls occasionally escaping him. When I headed for the front door he pranced ahead, certain that he could take on the noisy creature and win.

A Public Works truck, towing an equipment trailer, was pulled up at the curb in front of Bridget's house. Being maneuvered off the trailer was a vehicle that looked like the offspring of a bulldozer and a bumper car, with a toothy scoop carried jauntily overhead. The driver guided it down from the trailer and over to Bridget's driveway. He wore the orange vest and hard hat of the city worker.

Corky appeared beside me, rubbing the sleep out of his eyes. He stared at the little bulldozer. "A Bobcat! Cool!"

"Bobcat?" I bent close to make sure I'd heard correctly over the noise. Corky wasn't waiting around to talk to me, though.

"Sam!" He ran back to his room, oblivious to my hushing. "Sam! There's a Bobcat in our driveway!"

Sam bounded off his bunk bed and thudded out to the front door. Luckily he didn't wake Mick, and I heard nothing from Moira. Crossing my fingers, I shut the boys' door again and joined them on the front porch.

The Public Works man got out of the Bobcat and climbed back into the truck that towed the trailer. He drove away.

"Cool!" Corky cried. "He's giving it to us!"

He was crushed when the driver, after parking the truck farther up the street, came striding back.

The boys poured down the front walk toward him.

"Hey, mister! Is that your Bobcat?"

"Can I drive?"

Corky turned on Sam. "Don't be stupid," he said witheringly. "You don't have a lionsense." He turned back to the Public Works man. "Can I help you drive?"

"Are you going to scoop up all the bones?"

The man blinked at the onslaught. "Are you the ones that made all this trouble?"

Corky and Sam stopped short, looking down at the ground. They didn't reply.

The man saw me standing on the porch and smiled. "Guess you've already given them hell over causing this mess."

"Not really." I couldn't help the frosty note in my voice. "After all, they did accomplish a public service."

"Ma'am?" The man stared at me. Corky and Sam, sensing that they weren't going to be yelled at, moved closer to the alluring machinery. "Hold on, fellas. No unauthorized personnel allowed in the Bobcat." He relented a little at their disappointed faces. "But I will let you sit in it before the dump truck comes and I have to get to work."

"A dump truck is coming to our house?" Sam's eyes got even bigger.

"That's right." He swung Sam into the driver's seat of the Bobcat. I came down to stand beside the mound of dirt.

"Are you going to dig up the bones?" I wondered if Drake knew about this.

He shrugged, lifting Sam down and helping Corky to climb up. "I got orders to come out and pick up this debris, so that's what I'm doing." Corky's delighted manipulation of the levers that bristled out of the control panel made him smile. "The youngsters sure get a bang out of trucks and such, don't they, ma'am?"

"It's kind of you to let them experience it." I glanced back over my shoulder, wondering if Moira was crying inside. "Did you know that a police investigation is going on here?"

"Don't know anything about that," he said. "Just got my orders, that's all." He glanced around. "Nowadays, this neighborhood doesn't seem like it needs the police so much. People have sure fixed up the houses."

"I believe a lot of remodeling has gone on." I didn't mention Bridget's house, which was still in an unremodeled state.

The Public Works guy looked at it. I read the name patch on his shirt: STEWART. He was fortyish, stout around the middle but strong-looking. He took off his hard hat, giving me a look at his curly fringe of gray-black hair around a tanned, receding hairline.

"Now that house," Stewart continued, nodding behind me to Bridget's place. "I see nobody's fixed it up. Looks just the same as it used to."

"You know this house?"

"I've been in it before, back in my salad days. Grew up in Palo Alto. Not here," he said, his lip curling just a little. "This

44

was the tough part of town when I was a kid. I grew up in Evergreen Park." He said it as if Evergreen Park was a separate community several miles away, but it was another Palo Alto neighborhood, not a mile away as the crow flies. "We didn't come over here often, unless we was looking for a fight."

"I heard there were a lot of hippies and people like that living around here."

"That was later, about the time I knew this house." He winked at me. "I didn't go to Stanford, but I knew some of those students. We had us some parties. This was one big party house for a while."

A dump truck rumbled up and parked in front of the driveway. The driver jumped out and shambled toward Stewart. He was tall, with movements that seemed lanky and uncoordinated. He, too, wore a shirt with a name patch; his said DOUG. Something about his face disturbed me. Although he appeared to be in his early forties, like Stewart, his face seemed to lack the carvings of experience's knife. The expression he turned to Stewart was anxious, exaggeratedly so. Sam, watching his brother hog the Bobcat, had almost the same expression.

"Hey, Doug." Stewart's voice when he spoke to his coworker was gentle. "Just let this young man finish up, then we'll get to work."

Doug nodded several times. "We'll get to work. I'll drive the dump truck."

"That's right, buddy."

Doug looked at the dirt, at the shapes of the bones sticking out. His eyes widened.

"Stewart, what's that? That shouldn't be there."

I called Corky down from the Bobcat, and he came reluctantly. "You and Sam go back inside now," I said. I didn't want them focusing more on the bones. "Let me know if Moira's still asleep."

They went reluctantly, feet dragging, gazing over their shoulders at the object of their desire, the Bobcat.

"It's nothing, Doug," Stewart said, soothingly. "You get on back to the dump truck now." He turned to me. " 'Scuse me, ma'am. Gotta get started. We're on overtime, and the city don't want us to spend our time chatting."

I looked at Doug, climbing into the truck, and Stewart seemed to know what I was thinking.

"He's a very careful driver, ma'am. Just a little slow in taking stuff in sometimes."

"I'm sure he's fine." I felt a little ashamed of my knee-jerk reaction to Doug's disability. "But you really should check your orders again." Drake would have apoplexy when he knew that his bones were in danger from the city workers. "The police wanted someone to come and secure the site, not dig it up."

Stewart scratched his head. "Well—"

"I'll call the officer in charge. Can you wait until he comes? It won't be long."

"I'll talk to Doug about it." He looked dubious. "We're just doing what we're told, ma'am."

I trotted up the walk, meeting Corky and Sam on the front porch.

"Moira's still sleeping." Corky looked past me. "Can't we stay out here and see what they do?"

"Don't leave the porch, then. And tell me the minute they start digging."

I dialed Drake's number, and got his answering machine, but before I could leave a message he came on the line, panting.

"Some men are here from the city," I began.

"You got me out of the shower for that?"

"They have a Bobcat and a dump truck, and they're going to take everything away."

Drake's reaction was loud and colorful. I held the receiver away from my ear.

"Don't let them start," he said feverishly. "I'll be right there. Keep them from starting."

"You want me to throw my body in front of the Bobcat?" I spoke to the dial tone. Drake had hung up.

Stewart was still conferring with Doug when I went back out. Sam and Corky were arguing about how the scoop on the Bobcat worked. Sam went inside and came back out with *The Big Book of Trucks*. They put their heads together over this impressive reference work.

I went down to talk to the men. Shaking his head, Stewart climbed into the Bobcat's seat. "Sorry, ma'am," he said when I came closer. "Doug's work order says the same as mine—all debris to be removed. Even got a dump permit."

"I've spoken to the detective in charge. He doesn't want you to disturb the site." I pointed to the pieces of bone that stuck out of the pile. "Those are human bones. He thinks someone was deliberately buried there years ago, and the police have to make sure there was no foul play involved."

"A body!" Stewart seemed disbelieving. "Nobody said anything about this to Doug and me. We're just trying to do our jobs, ma'am. If you'd step aside?" He put on a pair of protective earmuffs and started up the Bobcat. The noise was terrific. The scoop clanked a warning.

Drake's battered car pulled up, nose-to-nose with the dump truck. He jumped out, waved me away, and charged around to Stewart's side, shouting something. Stewart shrugged, indicating the noise protectors he wore. Drake took out his ID folder and waved it in Stewart's face. I had rarely seen him in such a passion.

The racket stopped. I went back and opened the front door, so I could hear any sounds of waking from inside. Corky, Sam, and I kept Barker on the front porch by the simple expedient of sitting along the top step. I read from *The Big Book of Trucks*, learning more about diesel engines in the process than I had room for in my brain.

After intense negotiations, Drake pulled a cell phone out of his pocket and made a call, then gave the phone to Stewart, who talked for a while and then handed the phone back to Drake. The two men shook hands, then Stewart talked to Doug while Drake came toward the house. The dump truck rumbled away, much to Corky and Sam's dismay.

"Aren't they going to dump anything?"

"Aunt Liz, where's that Bobcat guy going?"

Stewart, ambling up the sidewalk toward the parked truck-trailer, waved at the boys. "Next time," he called. Drake gave him a tight smile. He didn't sit down on the steps until Stewart had reinstalled the Bobcat on the trailer and driven away.

Then he collapsed on the step below me. "Whew. Close call."

"What brought them out here, anyway?"

"Somebody got the wires crossed and issued a demolition permit instead of the work order I asked for." Drake smiled at me. "Thanks for being on top of it, Liz. I guess I'll just camp out here until we get this sewed up." He grinned at Corky and Sam. "I hear there are places around that bring Chinese food right to your house. How does that sound?"

It sounded fine to the boys. "It's not dinnertime yet, Drake."

"Believe me," he said, squeezing my hand gently before heading for the phone, "before I'm through here, it will be."

7 _____

DRAKE took over the kitchen. He took calls on his cell phone, made calls on Bridget's phone, and covered the kitchen table with a blizzard of notes scribbled on every loose bit of paper he could find.

I helped Corky and Sam in the living room. They were building a fort out of blankets draped over chairs and tables, reinforced with every pillow they could find.

Sam smoothed an afghan over the coffee table. "Under here is where the bones are," he told Corky.

Not being a card-carrying parent, I didn't know how to handle this. Would finding a skeleton do irreparable damage to their tender young minds? Should I engage them in thoughtful exploration of their feelings? Should I treat it all as some kind of Mister Rogers adventure? "Let's go visit Mr. Skeleton. Do you know how many bones are in your body?" I took the easy path and pretended I didn't hear any remarks not addressed to me.

While I was in the kitchen getting juice, the phone rang. Drake was talking away on his cell phone, so I answered.

"Liz!" It was Bridget. She sounded as if she were calling from right next door instead of across a wide expanse of ocean. "How is everything going?"

"Fine, Biddy. It's going fine." Drake lifted his head when I said her name. "How are you guys? Flight okay?"

"It was crowded," Bridget said, "and the cattle-car thing

definitely came to mind. But it's so beautiful here! We've already been for a walk on the beach, and we're going to have lunch pretty soon. This is a fabulous hotel. How are the kids?"

"They're fine." I turned my back on Drake, who was signaling something I couldn't interpret. "Moira and Mick are still napping. Corky and Sam and I are building a fort in the living room. Do you mind if they use the sofa cushions?"

"No, they can use whatever they want, so long as it isn't breakable and they put it back." Bridget's rich, warm laughter floated into the room, making me smile. "Say, the phone's been busy for a while. I was just about to give up until after lunch. What's going on?"

"Nothing." I gulped. "People are calling for you, mostly. And a couple of calls for the kids. It's hectic around here."

"This isn't going to be too much for you, is it, Liz?" Bridget sounded anxious. "I feel like I pretty much forced you to do it, but you'll be all right, won't you?"

"Sure I will." I tried to be soothing, something that's not natural for me. "And I have lots of help. Claudia took the boys downtown for milkshakes, and Melanie's already stopped over to make sure I'm not blowing it."

Bridget laughed again. "Melanie always thinks she's the only one who can do anything right. But if you need help, she's promised to stand by. In fact, she said she would take Moira on Tuesday and Thursday while the boys are in school. That should give you some time for yourself."

I was a little ashamed of my impatience toward Melanie, but not much. "And Drake's treating us to Chinese food tonight."

After a silence, Bridget said, "Drake's helping out, too? That's great." Her voice, almost as expressive as her face, was easy to read. Enthusiasm and speculation, blended about 60–40. She paused again. "Will he spend the night?"

"Of course not." I kept my back turned to Drake, knowing my face was flaming. "But Barker will."

"Oh, that's comparable."

I ignored this gentle sarcasm. "Anyway, everyone's fine here. Although," I added, to gratify a fond mother, "we had a little choking up after you left. They miss you, of course."

"I don't worry about the boys," Bridget said. "But Moira's been so clingy lately—"

"She's reveling in independence." I made my voice brisk because Bridget sounded shaky. Hard though it might be to believe, many parents seem to miss their small children when they're not around. "Have you been in that warm, wonderful ocean yet?"

"Not yet, but Emery's already checked out the scuba and sailboard rentals and booked us for a sunset cruise on the catamaran." Bridget was cheerful again. "I can't believe this is frugal us, just tossing our money around like plutocrats."

"Enjoy it. Take lots of pictures."

"I am." Another pause. "Well, do the boys want to speak to me?"

The boys would undoubtedly mention the bones if they spoke. "They're pretty busy now. How about we call you around bedtime? Will you be in?"

"I'll be in," Bridget vowed. She gave me their room number to add to the three pages of neatly typed instructions she'd left, and hung up.

"Good," Drake said. "You didn't tell her about the body." He put his cell phone on the table and stretched, yawning. "She might have cut short her vacation."

Drake has had a soft spot for Bridget ever since I met him. That didn't bother me. A lot of people felt the same, men and women. She brought out people's protective instincts, whether she needed to or not. I suppose it's nice that Drake gets crushes on regular women like Bridget and myself, who are far, very far, from being fashionably scrawny young twigs. In my own case, the beauty is pretty much internal, so whatever Drake was seeing was in the eye of the beholder.

These thoughts were dangerous. I had all too often lately

51

found myself analyzing Drake's seeming attraction to me. It was a short step from there to analyzing my own attraction to him.

I looked into the living room, where Corky and Sam dove in and out of blanket-shrouded hidey-holes, and pulled myself back to the conversation. "Bridget certainly deserves this vacation. Anyone who lives full-time with children does. It would be awful if she had to come home early."

"I guess." Drake looked vague. "I just didn't want her and Emery coming back and cluttering up my investigation." He grinned at me. "I know I can keep you in order."

"Why ever would you think so?" My exasperation wasn't totally feigned.

"Because you love a mystery. Confess, Liz. Why else would you get mixed up in them so often?"

"How exactly did I get mixed up in this one?" I resisted the impulse to wipe that smug smile off his face. This is the reason why I can't quite let myself be swept away by Drake. He can be so irritating. I think all men are, at least some of the time. Probably women are to men, too. I don't need the aggravation.

"You stirred it up somehow. Just think, if you hadn't let the boys dig, those bones would probably not have been discovered for decades longer."

"Nonsense. The city's been chewing up the sidewalks at an ever-increasing rate. Cable, storm drains, sewer replacements—seems like they're digging everything up constantly. They're digging up the middle of the street out there now, you may have noticed. They'd have run across the bones when they re-do the sidewalk again in six months or so."

"You're probably right." Drake picked up the cellular phone again. "Don't let me keep you."

I took the juice out to the living room, feeling deprived of the last word. There are many things about trying to sustain a relationship with a man that make me uncomfortable. My very need of the last word showed up a kind of competition with

Drake that I had noticed before. Perhaps I was only capable of cessation of hostilities in a relationship, not true love. I didn't like seeing things between men and women as a war.

The boys had abandoned their fort and were standing on the window seat, their noses plastered against the glass. "He's back!" Corky sounded ecstatic.

"There's no Bobcat, though."

I set the juice on top of the bookcase and joined them. Stewart, the Public Works guy, had returned, in a different truck with different accessories, which was double-parked in front of the driveway. We watched him rummage in the back of the truck and pull out a brilliant orange tarp. He flapped this toward the foot of the excavation, as if making a bed. After walking around to smooth it here and there, he put a portable barricade at each end and strung caution tape around. He stood off, surveying his work, and found it good. After a glance at the house, he drove away again.

Drake found us on the window seat, our noses still glued to the glass as we watched Stewart's truck disappear. I pointed out how tidy it was—the bones nicely tucked in, the site barricaded. Drake just sniffed.

"Our people would do a much better job." He flopped on the couch and closed his eyes, pressing his fingers into his forehead just above his eyebrows. "Trouble is, we're spread so thin this weekend. Training exercise in Mountain View, and a murder-suicide in East Palo Alto that Bruno's been detailed to help with. These bones have a very low priority, believe me." He sat up. "Much as I hate to, I've called in the archaeologists."

"Send in the clowns," I murmured.

Drake grinned. "Richard Grolen is kind of a clown, if you ask me. One of those overgrown types that never grows up. Still digging in the dirt. He's got to be over fifty."

"Not that old. And he seemed to be in good shape. Digging will do that for you, I guess."

Drake frowned. "I don't like giving it over to him, but

nobody in the department seems to feel these bones are of much interest, seeing how old they are. The county will send out a forensic anthropologist to date them, hopefully on Monday."

"I thought that's what Dinah Blakely was going to do."

"She'll want to sit in, probably, but it has to be official." Drake rumpled his hair. "And I guess I'll hang around over the weekend to keep tabs on the diggers. If I thought they wouldn't miss some evidence, I'd just let Public Works go for it." He sighed. "This looks like one enormous headache."

I didn't care for the way he looked at me when he said that. "Surely you don't blame me. Or was I just supposed to ignore what the boys had done? After all, the work crews would have noticed the bones on Monday, or at least what was left after the boys stirred it all up, anyway."

"No, no." He didn't sound convinced. "Of course, it's worth investigating. It'll just be so tedious to track down the ID at this late date, that's all."

"You call yourself a detective," I scoffed, helping Sam down from the window seat. "You have records, don't you? Who lived here, who was missing—"

"Liz." Drake was patient. "Those records are useful if you have a date. The forensic guys aren't going to say, 'This man was killed in August of 1975.' Without a benchmark in time of some kind, it's going to be damned difficult, even with our databases."

Moira woke just then, and by the time I'd tended her, Mick was awake. Drake ordered Chinese delivered, since he was expecting the archaeologists any time. I put *The Little Mermaid* in the VCR, reflecting that I'd allowed Bridget's children to watch far more TV that day than I really approved of. It was easy to see how moms got into letting the kids veg out in front of the tube.

Richard Grolen and his crew showed up at the same time as the Chinese food. He and Drake held a brief discussion, standing by the sidewalk. They shook hands like prizefighting opponents.

I cut some potstickers into tiny bites and let Moira sit on the floor with the boys in front of the TV while eating. Barker, especially, thought this was a fine idea.

Drake and I took our chopsticks and mu shu onto the front porch. We sat on the steps with the front door open behind us. I could hear the kids shrieking with laughter as Louie the Crab conducted an undersea orchestra. In front of us, the students lifted away the barricades and tarp, following Richard's directions.

"This better not be a mistake," Drake said around a bite. He caught a noodle that slithered off. "It could cost me in the department. The captain really wanted to wait until the county team has time to deal with it, but that could be weeks. I want this cleaned up."

"So do I." I thought of Bridget coming back to a full-scale excavation of dubious bones in her front yard. It was enough to destroy the benefit of any vacation.

Drake knew what I was thinking about. "It may not be done in a week. Depends on how fast these people move, and they don't usually move very fast. Grolen said they'd skimp a bit on the preliminaries, seeing that the layers have already been disturbed."

We sat there until we were finished eating, watching the students impose a grid on the site, then take pictures, then finally begin to dig, or rather, to remove dirt with hand trowels and buckets. I checked occasionally on the kids. Moira ate quite a bit of potsticker and beef with broccoli; nobody admitted feeding Barker, but he had the look of a satisfied dog. Twilight came, and deepening dusk.

Finally Richard Grolen came over to the steps to fill Drake in on the progress so far, leaving his crew to pack up the bones they'd unearthed. I could see that I wasn't wanted in the official consultation, so I wandered down to the sidewalk. It occurred to me that no one had offered the students anything to drink. "Say, if you guys are thirsty—"

"I wouldn't say no to a Coke," one of the men said. He was short, with a round face reddened by the work he'd been doing. His baseball cap was turned backwards, shading his neck, and his eyes were magnified by thick-lensed glasses.

"Geez, Nelson," said the female member of the crew, pushing her hat farther back on her head. "You brought a cooler full of drinks. You already empty that?"

"I don't have any Coke," I said, hoping to cool the altercation. "But I could get you some ice water."

"That's nice," the girl said, wiping her grimy hand on her jeans and extending it to me. "I'm Kathy Swenson, by the way." Despite the hat, her nose was going to peel. Her pale blue eyes were ringed by pale blond lashes. "This is Hobart Pena, and that bottomless pit over there is Nelson Drabble. We'll be going soon anyway. Thanks for your offer, though."

Nelson looked like he wanted to argue with her, but Hobart gave me a languid nod and turned away. He was a handsome young fellow, with jet-black hair and bronzed skin. His brief T-shirt displayed muscles worth looking at.

Certainly Kathy looked at them, although with what appeared to be abstract appreciation. She was tall, skinny to the point of boniness, and her pale skin wasn't taking the sun well.

"Well, let me know if you need a drink. And you're welcome to take your breaks on the front porch where it's shady, as long as you're quiet at naptime." I smiled at Kathy, sure that she at least would understand this.

"That's very nice. We don't usually get any perks on the dig," Kathy said frankly, glancing at the front porch where Drake and Richard Grolen still conferred. Grolen looked over at the same time, and she got back to work.

I went back to the porch. Grolen gave me a smile, but without the extra charm he'd turned on for Melanie, and walked down the steps toward the crew. They heaved the last couple of tools into their van and drove away.

"So far they've found just a few bones," Drake said with gloomy satisfaction. "Our guys would have gotten all the bones by now."

"Did they find any bullets or anything?"

He showed me the little cardboard box Richard had given him. In it were some rusty Matchbox cars and a few bits of broken glass. "That's it," he said. "Doesn't look too lethal." He carried the box down to his car anyway. "Is there any more of that mu shu?"

After we cleared away the dinner, Drake read to the boys while I got Moira cleaned up. She asked for Mommy a couple of times, but at least she didn't cry when I told her Mommy was visiting and would be home later. Despite her long nap, she was asleep soon after I started rocking her.

Feeling like a manipulator, I told the boys we were going to call their parents. "It's expensive," I said. "We can't talk long. What should we tell them?"

"About the Bobcat!" Corky was firm.

"And the dump truck," Sam added.

"Okay, we can talk about the road construction. What about your trip to the Peninsula Creamery?"

"Yes, we had beer!" Sam licked his lips, remembering.

We made the call, and between the boys both talking at once on separate extensions and Bridget getting so excited to hear from them, the bones weren't mentioned. Emery did ask about the dump truck, and Sam told him, with great disappointment, that the men hadn't dumped the bones in it. But Corky was off on a tangent immediately, and Emery didn't follow up on it.

When we hung up, I was limp with relief.

Drake tucked the boys in, then came out to the living room. "That was fun," he said. "Haven't read *Mike Mulligan and His Steam Shovel* in several decades."

I dropped into a chair. "I'm exhausted."

"No wonder." He stood behind me and rubbed my neck and shoulders. It felt good. "You've had a very hard day."

"Tomorrow has to be better, though." I let my head fall forward. "Unless the kids discover a toxic waste site or something. And Monday they go to school all day."

"Poor Liz." His hands rotating over my shoulders did amazing things to my insides. "At least I'll be around tomorrow."

"I may not." He stopped rubbing, and I sat up. "I was thinking about taking the kids somewhere. Then you and Richard could dig to your hearts' content."

"Might be a good idea."

"But only if you're going to be here. I can't abandon Biddy's house to those archaeologists."

"I'll be here." He began to smile. "So you're going to take four kids on an excursion single-handed? That's brave."

"Claudia might go with me." I stood up. "And I'll need my rest."

Drake took the hint. I walked him to the door, and he kissed me before he left. He'd been doing that for a little while now. It was getting harder and harder to pretend these were just California kisses between friends.

Nevertheless, after he'd gone, I did pretend that. I phoned Claudia, who agreed to go with us on an expedition the next day. Then I walked around the house, accompanied by Barker, locking all the doors and turning out lights.

I was keyed up, not ready to sleep. Bridget and Emery had bookcases everywhere, bulging with books. Emery's books on solid-state-this and algorithm-that didn't interest me. But Bridget's books were like a smorgasbord to a dieter. I chose *Villette* to take into bed with me, and only for a minute or two did I think about a different choice I could have made.

8

I got up early to pack everything I could find to eat into a knapsack, along with Bridget's family membership card for the California Academy of Sciences in Golden Gate Park, thoughtfully included with her pages of instructions.

I made pancakes for breakfast, not quite up to Bridget's standards, but the boys didn't seem to notice. Halfway through the second batch, Barker left his post under the kitchen table and raced to the front door, ears alert. Corky ran into the living room and climbed on the window seat. "Those arkenologists are back!"

Sam abandoned his pancakes to climb up beside his brother. "They're digging up our bones again!"

I stood behind them, looking at the battered white van. "They're down to the sidewalk level already. Probably removing what you guys did was the easy part." Drake's car pulled up. He hopped out, gave Richard a curt nod, and headed up the front walk.

"I don't wanna go to the museum," Corky whined with his nose plastered to the window. "I wanna stay and help them dig."

Drake walked in in time to hear this. "That's all I need," he said.

"Relax. We're leaving." I crammed a bottle of juice and a stack of little paper cups into the knapsack. "But Barker's staying. Can you keep an eye on him? He likes to dig, too."

"I'm in charge of an investigation here," Drake said, "not dog-sitting."

"Okay, I'll stop by my place and lock him up for the day."

Drake sighed. "Leave him here. I don't want to be responsible for more phone calls about his howling."

"He doesn't howl much anymore."

"If that's what you think, it's lucky for you I'm in a position to squash the neighbors' complaints."

I hefted the knapsack. "Okay, does anyone need to go to the bathroom before we leave?"

The boys ignored me. Moira, I already knew, was dry.

It took four trips back and forth before all the kids and equipment were loaded into Bridget's rusty old Suburban. I would have driven my own equally rusty VW bus, but it didn't have enough space for all the equipment.

The Suburban was a whole new driving experience for me. I lumbered it carefully down the driveway, managing not to hit any of the digging students. The Public Works crew was putting in overtime down the block, crunching through some more asphalt. I waved at Stewart, and he and Doug waved back.

We threaded through cool, leafy streets. Palo Alto wore Sunday morning quiet; the sidewalks downtown were only crowded around the coffee and bagel shops. On an impulse I stopped at the Bagel Works. The kids fell on the warm cinnamon-raisin bagels with enthusiasm.

Claudia, too, appreciated the cup of coffee I'd brought her in a to-go cup with a lid. She settled herself in the passenger seat and accepted responsibility for tending Moira and Mick, strapped into car seats on the middle bench. The older boys occupied the back bench, along with an indestructible-looking tape recorder, a pile of cassette tapes and Tintin books, a box of coloring books and crayons, and enough Legos to build a whole city.

That Suburban was like a yacht. There was room behind the

third bench seat for the rest of it: stroller, bulging diaper bag for Moira, change of clothes for both Mick and Moira in case of accident, everyone's warm jacket in case it was cold in San Francisco, the knapsack of food, and the Suburban's toolbox, which I desperately hoped not to need. I can keep my old bus running because I know it so well. I didn't have a clue about Bridget's car.

Claudia sipped noisily at her coffee and took a bagel from the bag on the front seat. "This is a great idea," she said, glancing behind her. "Keep the little mouths full, and they're much quieter."

"It won't last." I headed for 280, the more scenic route to San Francisco. "Thanks for agreeing to come, Claudia. I'm just not up to handling four kids in a museum by myself."

"Who is?" Claudia turned toward me. "I didn't come because I'm so nice, Liz, so don't waste your thanks on me. I came to hash over the bones."

I checked the rearview mirror to see the kids' reaction to this. None of them appeared to be able to hear what we said in the front seat. Corky and Sam were barely visible way in back, their heads together over the tape recorder. Faint strains of Ray Stevens drifted up to us. In the middle seat, Mick munched steadily through his bagel. Moira wasn't eating the piece of bagel clutched in her chubby fist; she had already succumbed to road hypnosis.

"Okay, what about the bones?"

Claudia wriggled herself more comfortably into the seat. She enjoyed second-guessing Drake about any of his cases, but especially the occasional suspicious death. In her opinion, he didn't apply the scholarly method. "What have you learned from Drake?"

"Nothing, really. He just wants to get them dug up and hopes to figure out who it is."

My peripheral vision glimpsed Claudia's huge, Chessy-cat smile. "I know who it is."

61

"Claudia!" The Suburban bumped over a couple of lane markers before I wrenched it back into line. "How on earth—"

"I don't know his name, of course." Claudia shrugged off this minor detail. "But I thought about it all evening, and when I talked to Melanie, I knew."

"Melanie? What does she have to do with it?"

"Oh, nothing with the crime, I'm sure." Claudia waved one massive arm with half-eaten bagel attached. I ducked. "But she was there, you know, for a couple of years. She lived in that house. That's where I first met her. In fact, she baby-sat for Carlie and Jack a couple of times, after our first sitter proved so unreliable. I knew her folks, of course, or I would never have trusted another hippie."

"Melanie was a hippie!" It seemed so unlikely that perfect Melanie could ever have worn torn jeans and love beads.

"Oh, maybe she was more of a wanna-be, but she was there." Claudia considered for a minute, munching. "Actually, she's had trouble with drugs. Didn't you know?"

I shook my head. Gossiping makes me uncomfortable. It seems so unfair, somehow. Claudia loves to gossip, excusing it on the grounds that it's not gossip unless you're judgmental; otherwise it's just research into the vagaries of human behavior.

And I did have a rank little need to hear anything shady about Melanie, who wanted everyone to do good the way she thought was best. Every time I refused to volunteer in one of those society-type charities that target the homeless population, she let me feel her disapproval. I do what I can on a one-to-one basis with characters like Old Mackie, who often drops by for a meal and was just then the proud possessor of my favorite pair of thick wool socks. But I don't want to stand there and flaunt my good luck in having a house over people who used to be my neighbors on the street.*

* Murder in a Nice Neighborhood

So I didn't stop Claudia from telling me about Melanie's checkered past.

"Yes, awhile ago—it would be about the time Biddy got pregnant with Moira—Melanie was mixed up in a murder case. She ended up in Betty Ford kicking a nasty cocaine habit, and since then she's been so holier-than-thou. Wants to pretend she was never a hell-raiser, never used an illegal substance." Claudia made a noise between a sniff and a snort. "I wasn't taking any of that, you can believe. Asked her who she bought her drugs from back in the old days."

I checked the rearview mirror again. Mick had joined Moira in bye-bye land. Sam and Corky were having a delightful time with Ray Stevens. Already, after little more than twenty-four hours in their company, I knew they would move on to Weird Al Yankovic soon.

"What did she say?"

Claudia laughed. "You mean after she denied using drugs? That was funny. I had to remind her that I had been in that house in the seventies, I knew what all those kids were doing. That Richard Grolen, for instance. Soon as I laid eyes on him, I remembered him. He was older than the rest of them, but no better. Alfred and I came home once and found Melanie entertaining him in the living room."

"You mean—"

"Necking." She said the word with zest. "In fact, petting. Yes! *Heavy* petting. Of course, the kids were asleep, and no harm done. But when I reminded Melanie of that, she stopped weaseling. She said she didn't remember the real name of that fellow who was the dealer. They called him Nado, because he came from Kansas and he kept talking about tornadoes all the time. He just vanished the year she graduated. Nobody really paid much attention, but she remembers because she wanted some dope or something for a party and couldn't find this guy anywhere, and that's when people started wondering what happened to him. They figured he was in jail somewhere."

"Maybe he was."

"He was never seen again." Claudia's voice was low and portentous. "Now, considering that most of those people have turned up, off and on, over the years, don't you think that's suspicious? I mean, take Richard Grolen. He's been gone for a while, but here he is, back again. Melanie, some of the others—they're still around town. I see them every now and again. Saw that ex-baby-sitter of mine at a Red Ribbon Week rally, urging her kids to say no to drugs." Claudia laughed again. "That tickled me. I almost went up and asked her if she was drawing from her own experience."

"People change."

"That they do," Claudia agreed with good humor. "That's what makes them so interesting."

We were silent for a moment. "So you think this drug dealer overreached himself in some way and was killed and buried beneath the sidewalk."

"Melanie couldn't remember if the sidewalk was torn up just then or not," Claudia said, sounding disgruntled.

"Who could? It must be fifteen years or more since then."

"At least fifteen years. But it narrows it down a good deal."

"This is total speculation." I glanced at Claudia, who was working on her second bagel. "You have no basis for any of this."

"I have a feeling," Claudia said darkly. "And at least I'm looking around. Your Drake is so involved with digging up the here and now he can't be bothered to dig up the past."

"He'll get there." I had another thought. "Did you tell him any of this?"

"He'd be even less inclined than you to believe it."

I had to agree that was true. "Nevertheless, he should know. And I don't think you should go asking around anymore, Claudia. You might provoke someone."

"You think Melanie is the killer?" Claudia chuckled. "I don't think so. She doesn't have the guts."

"She might spread it around that you're interested, though. The killer might hear—" I caught myself.

"If it's all a crock, as you just said, there's no danger, is there?" Claudia stared at me with bright, amused eyes. "And if it's not, then any interest in me is proof I'm on the right track."

"Would that be any satisfaction if the killer comes after you?" I shivered. "That is not a pleasant experience."

Claudia patted my arm. "Just be thankful you aren't mixed up in it this time, Liz. I'm not in any danger just from poking around. Heavens, I don't even know any of their names, except Melanie's. I didn't remember Richard's name until I met him again. Most of them went by nicknames anyway. That flaky baby-sitter called herself Primrose. I think her real name is Jane Holfinger. There was another one they called Mondo Man, and a girl named Wendy, I think. Don't know any of the rest of them, and believe me, they came and went. That house must have seen upwards of twenty young people in the space of a year."

"Drake ought to know, anyway."

"You're so loyal." Claudia made me sound a bit like Barker. I wondered if he was giving Drake a hard time. I wished that Bridget's mom hadn't broken her ankle. I wished that Emery hadn't chosen this week to have a conference in Hawaii. I wished I were holed up in my cottage, peacefully writing about winter aconites for *Ornamental Horticulture*.

"Anyway," Claudia said, "Melanie agreed to tell Drake whatever she knew."

"Maybe she's in danger, too."

Claudia sounded impatient. "No one's in danger now, Liz. This all happened so long ago. If it turns out to be this drug dealer under the sidewalk, he might even have died of an overdose and panicked someone into planting him there. Whoever did it is probably long gone now."

"Maybe not." I slowed for a turn onto Brotherhood Way that would take us the back way into Golden Gate Park, avoiding the traffic on 19th. "You just pointed out that all those people turn up again, and some of them never left." I shook it off. "This is all stupid, anyway. No way could you come up with the identity of those bones just from gossiping with Melanie."

"You're probably right." Claudia sounded disappointed. "So Drake shouldn't know. He's so competitive about his cases."

"*He* is?" I smothered a laugh.

We managed to find a place to park not too far from the museum and marched our troops inside, where there were bones enough to please everyone. However, when I had my turn at a bathroom break, I found a pay phone and left a message for Drake about Claudia's revelations. I didn't go into detail—didn't have that much change. But I felt he should know.

9

WE had meant to have our picnic on Ocean Beach, but the wind blew a cloud of fine sand over the beach right at sandwich level if you were sitting on a blanket. So we spent a few minutes looking at the few hardy souls sailboarding in that cold water, located a sea lion or two, and then took our lunch to Queen Wilhelmina's Tulip Garden by the north windmill. The tulips were long gone, of course, but a vivid display of zinnias and petunias took their place, and the windmill proved interesting to the boys.

On the way home, everyone slept, even Claudia, whose soft snores began soon after we wheeled onto 280. I felt a little guilty for dragging her all over the Academy of Sciences. Standing in the middle of the Fish Surround, a circular room with walls made from a continuous fish tank, watching the leopard sharks and salmon and rockfish and groupers swimming by had made all of us dizzy, but Claudia had had to sit down.

I didn't mind that my passengers were snoozing, especially when the "Riders in the Sky" tape ended and no little fingers pushed the rewind button. There's only so much yodeling a person can take. In the quiet, with just engine noise to distract me, I started thinking about what Claudia had said earlier.

I found Melanie Dixon irritating, but she was in a bad position if Claudia were right. Anyone who came within the boundaries of a criminal investigation had my sympathy. I was just glad Bridget was well out of it. She would have been aghast at the trouble her house had gotten into—still would be, when she returned. If only Drake could clean up the investigation by then.

I turned it over in my mind, wondering how you could ever learn the details about something that had happened so long ago. Even if the bones could be firmly identified, reconstructing the last few hours or days of that person's life would be nearly impossible. Anyone whose movements were noticed enough to be recollected would also have been missed at the time.

Drake didn't talk about his job to me, and I didn't want to know about police work, but I wondered how they searched for old information. This is a subject I know something about, having written a couple of articles on Palo Alto history for *Smithsonian*. I decided to do some checking of my own the next day, Monday. The boys would be in school, leaving only Moira to tend. Surely she and I could do some library work without too much hassle.

Claudia started yawning and blinking when I turned off 280 at Sand Hill. The kids slept until we pulled into the driveway.

Or rather, tried to pull into the drive. It was occupied at the time—not by a car or truck, but by Drake and Richard Grolen. They stood in the middle of the drive, heads thrust toward each other, fists clenched, like male-aggression poster boys. The students watched incredulously, as if unable to believe that people so old could still put up their dukes. Even Stewart had left his crew and was standing nearby, his expression bemused.

Claudia leaned forward. "Now, what's this? The menfolk are squaring off."

"But why?" I wondered if I should park on the street.

"Melanie, probably," Claudia said. Melanie was there, fluttering around, pulling at Richard's arm, pushing at Drake. Dinah Blakely, too, stood on the front steps, her hands to her mouth as she watched the men. Richard had a good four inches on Drake, who's not that tall for a man, although he towers over me. Drake was younger, but he didn't have those shovel-lifting muscles that us girls had been admiring in Richard the day before.

Appalled to find myself measuring them as opponents, I honked the horn. For a long moment, neither man moved. Then, reluctantly, they stepped apart.

Melanie came running over to the passenger door before I even got the car parked. "Where have you been?" She was beside herself. "How could you just go away and leave that— that savage in charge?"

"I didn't think he was so combative when I met him yesterday." I set the Suburban's parking brake. The middle-seat kids slumbered on, but Corky and Sam watched the drama, wide-eyed. They were more used to their own brand of fighting.

"Melanie means Detective Drake, don't you?" Claudia fished around on the front seat and assembled her purse, the bag of bagels, and the various pamphlets she'd collected during our excursion. "What's the fight about?"

"Oh, it's terrible." Melanie's distress was evident; her mascara was streaked, her lipstick gnawed away. "Richard and his crew had found a lot of the bones and put them on the lawn in some kind of order. Then they went to lunch. After all, a policeman was here, even if he was too busy to come out and help them." She darted a glare over her shoulder at Drake. "When the crew came back from lunch, the bones were gone."

"That is terrible."

"And the oh-so-alert policeman didn't even notice."

"Be fair." Dinah Blakely entered the conversation, coming down the steps. "Nobody thought to tell Paul we were leaving. It was kind of careless."

"Kind of careless?" Drake shook his head. His hair was wild, a sure sign of excessive perturbation. "Evidence in a possible homicide! And after you'd agreed to follow procedure!"

69

He glared at Richard. "I ought to arrest you for obstructing an investigation." His gaze swept Kathy, Nelson, and Hobart, who huddled together on the sidewalk, Dinah Blakely, and Richard.

To his credit, Richard backed away from the confrontation. "Look, Drake—" His hands unclenched. "It's true. I blew it. I should have taken better care—"

"It's not Dr. Grolen's fault." Nelson stepped forward, pushed perhaps by the other two. He was wearing sunglasses with thick prescription lenses. "I brought my lunch today, and I said I'd stay with the bones. But—" he swallowed. "I—I started thinking about ice cream, and figured I could get downtown and back in no time. I just didn't think to let Detective Drake know. It seemed so busy here with the road crew and all, I never thought anyone would just come up and walk off with the bones. Guess I didn't think at all."

"As usual," Kathy said brutally under her breath. Nelson's ears turned red.

"We would have been glad to keep an eye out, if you'd let us know," Stewart put in. "Sorry to say we didn't see anything unusual. But we were concentrating on our trench."

"At least the bone-nappers didn't get this." Richard Grolen pulled a tissue-wrapped object out of his pocket. Tenderly he folded back the paper, showing a curved piece of bone with three discolored teeth attached to it.

We all moved a little closer. Drake asked, "What's that?"

"Jawbone." Richard gazed down at it fondly. "With molars! Look at those roots. And a filling! Makes it easier to identify the body, if that's a concern of yours." He grinned at Dinah Blakely. "Also good from the anthropological point of view."

"Now, Richard!" Dinah Blakely laughed, sounding coy. Melanie's eyes narrowed, going from Dinah to Richard. "Given that the bones are modern, I doubt this person ate enough stone-ground corn to wear down his enamel, or carried a burden sling in his teeth."

"You've already figured out a few things, though. Right?" Richard made room for Dinah at his side.

"Well, I thought whoever it was might have been a nervous, uptight kind of person," she said, diffidently. "See, looks like he did grind his teeth. Pretty noticeably, since he was under twenty-five."

"How do you know that?" Drake had his untidy little notebook out, scrawling things down. He hovered over the jaw fragment in Richard's hand, as if he didn't trust the archaeologist not to whisk it away.

"It's a guess, really." Dinah Blakely was apologetic. "You can't really be totally sure about things in forensic anthropology. We know the approximate age because the growth plates had fused in the long bones, but there was little sign of stress and wear and tear."

"Of course, we can't substantiate that anymore, because the long bones were stolen." Drake kept his voice level.

I ran up the front steps. "Not all of them." The cardboard box rattled when I pushed it along the porch. "There are these ones, that the boys found."

Corky and Sam tumbled out of the car. "Yeah, we found some," Corky assured Richard.

Sam turned big blue eyes on Dinah Blakely. "Please, can we dig now? We'll find you some more bones."

An unmarked car pulled up in front of the house, and Drake welcomed his partner, Bruno Morales. Bruno waved cheerfully at me and at Claudia before going into a huddle with Drake. Claudia simply stood by the car, enjoying the scene and listening idly while Melanie poured a constant stream of what sounded like complaint into her ear. Stewart lingered, his interested gaze going from the box of bones to the sidewalk excavation.

Drake took Bruno over to the box of bones, and they listed them together, Drake in his notebook and Bruno on a small computer. Richard joined them, followed by Dinah. Sensing

71

that tension had lessened, Kathy and Hobart starting talking, pointedly excluding Nelson. He kicked idly at the tarp that covered the dig site, then took some chewing gum out of his pocket and offered it to the other students.

"Okay," Drake said finally. "Have we got it straight, Grolen? I don't have the manpower to put a uniform on the job here. You'll have to keep track of the bones, and when you're done tonight I'll take charge of them. We've inventoried, so we know what we have."

"It's starting to make a picture," Dinah Blakely chirped. "Male, six feet or thereabouts, probably slender build, nervous, had broken his femur a couple of years previously—probably a skiing accident. Oh, he also got into fights."

Melanie and Richard exchanged a long look.

Bruno Morales focused on Dinah. "Why do you say that?"

"Well," she said, flushing a little at his interest, "I guess now that the bones are stolen it's not really evidence. But we found the bones of his right hand all together, almost articulated. And there was some damage to the knuckles, not as pronounced as it would be in a professional pugilist, you understand, but pretty unmistakable. He'd slugged a few people in his time. It had to have hurt."

Drake had the bright idea of asking her to sketch what she'd seen, before the memory of it disappeared. He and Morales bustled her into the house, and the boys trailed along, totally enthralled with all this talk of skeletons and bones. Claudia followed them, mumbling about coffee. Stewart wandered back to his crew.

I climbed into the Suburban to liberate my youngest passengers from their restraints, not that they cared. Moira was still deeply asleep, and Mick was just starting to open his eyes. I fumbled with the unfamiliar buckles and straps, not wanting him to get vocal and wake up his sister. Then I heard Melanie talking, and realized that Richard must have joined her in leaning against the Suburban's rear fender. Either they didn't see me between the seats, or they didn't realize that the window behind them was open, broadcasting their low-voiced conversation into the car.

"Sounded familiar, didn't it?" Richard spoke first.

"I don't know what you mean." Melanie's lighter voice was easy to hear. Crouched in front of Mick, I could see her profile. She held her shoulders rigid.

"Sure you do, Mel." Richard's low rumble was harder to distinguish. "I could tell, when Dinah said that about the fist-fights. Looks like he finally got into trouble he couldn't get out of. Remember that time he cut the LSD with something that caused that guy to go catatonic?"

"Look, it's all conjecture." Melanie's voice was taut. "Nobody really knows any of those things, and with the bones gone—"

"Ah, yes, the bones. That was a little drastic, wasn't it? And futile, as it turns out. You should have remembered the box on the porch."

"I should have—" Melanie swung around and stared at him. "What do you mean? I didn't steal those bones. I don't care if they find out who it was. It has nothing to do with me."

"Doesn't it?" Richard sounded almost caressing. "Well, maybe not. Funny, though, isn't it. The past coming home to roost."

This interesting conversation held me motionless, but Mick brought it to an end by loudly demanding his freedom. Struggling once more with the buckles, I heard Richard striding toward the steps. Then Melanie pushed in beside me.

"Do you know how to do this?" I turned to her, keeping my face as bland as possible. "It's driving me crazy."

"Like this." She unsnapped and unstrapped with her usual brisk efficiency. "Did you hear what Richard and I were talking about?"

Where Melanie is involved, all my instincts for self-

73

preservation—and they are many—come directly to the surface.

"Were you talking?" I helped Mick out of the car seat and he gathered up his blanket in his arms. "Would you mind taking him into the house while I get Moira? She might sleep a little more if I put her right in her crib."

Melanie sniffed. "You wish." She smiled down at Mick. "Let's go find some juice."

Mick was agreeable. I draped Moira over my shoulder, reflecting on Melanie's odd combination of excellent mothering skills and her more annoying ways around grownups. I tried to memorize the conversation I'd heard, for later retelling to Drake. Of course, it would have been more dignified to admit I'd eavesdropped and challenge her to do something about it. However, the path of least resistance was mine.

10

THE kitchen bulged with people when I came in after putting Moira down. Claudia plopped the teakettle on the burner and rummaged through the tins that lined the stove's warming shelf, questing for coffee. The boys guzzled juice at one side of the big round table, while Drake and Morales conferred across from them. Dinah and Richard stood together, facing Melanie.

"Must you go?" Melanie, still holding the juice pitcher, fixed her gaze on Richard, and her words were less a question than a command. "I thought we could talk about it some more."

"No more to say." Richard smiled charmingly at her. "Ready, Dinah?"

I saw them to the door, wresting my hostess duties from Melanie. She had to hurry back to the kitchen to quiet the boys' demands for more juice.

Claudia, finding only coffee beans instead of the instant she prefers, gave up. "I'm going home to finish my nap," she declared. "It's too exciting for an old woman like me around here." She took the juice pitcher from Melanie and handed it to me. "You'll have to give me a ride, Melanie. Liz picked me up this morning."

"Oh, that's right." The Suburban had been seeking its home driveway and carried me blindly along with it.

Claudia tugged on Melanie's arm. "Anyway, your family will be wondering what's happened to you."

Melanie went, reluctantly. "Remember, I'm taking Moira on Tuesday and Thursday, and you're picking up Amanda when you get the boys after school tomorrow and Wednesday."

"It's very nice of you. Thanks." It was nice, since I would be able to teach my writing workshop Tuesday without worrying about Bridget's offspring.

"I told Bridget I would," Melanie said, making it clear whom the favor was for.

When they were gone, the kitchen seemed much quieter, even with three boys in it. I sat down at the table, my breath whooshing out.

"It's draining, isn't it?" Bruno smiled at me sympathetically. "I didn't know you would be brave enough to take on staying with children while their parents are away." His gaze turned speculative. "Do you do this often?"

"Never again," I said, wishing that my own juice was something stronger.

Bruno's face fell. Drake laughed. "Too bad, Bruno. I know you're anxious to get your missus off to yourself somewhere and create a fourth little Morales, but you'll have to find someone else to baby-sit. Liz is wasting away here."

"I can still listen, anyway." I told them about the conversation I'd overheard, and they both took notes, Drake in his tiny paper-spewing notebook, and Bruno very neatly on his small computer.

"It fits in with what Claudia told you. Melanie knows more than she's telling about what happened here, for sure." Drake, frowning, scrawled something else in his notebook.

"We must get more complete statements from all these people at once." Bruno pushed back his chair and stood up.

Drake agreed. "You do it, Bruno. I've been slaving away on this case all weekend, and I promised to bring pizza over here tonight."

The boys broke into a chant of "Pizza! Pizza!"

Bruno looked from Drake to me, smiling. "Yes, of cou[ ]
You do that, Paolo. Enjoy your taste of family life. Maybe you
will find it so agreeable you'll want more of it."

"He can have my share." It came out with a lot more feeling
than I realized. Bruno looked chagrined.

Drake laughed. "You'll feel better after something to eat.
Pizza with everything?"

I shuddered.

Bruno closed his notebook computer. "I will go, before you
make me hungry. Perhaps I'll have a name to put on those
bones by morning. We don't want the police to be the last to
know, do we?"

They made plans for the next day, while I went in to Moira,
whose nap had been ended by the pizza chant. Drake phoned
the pizza order in as soon as Bruno left, and the boys were gra-
cious enough to help clear the kitchen table of extraneous cups
and glasses while he went to pick it up.

It did help a great deal to have Drake there in the evening.
He kept the boys entertained pretty well by telling them all
about weapons training, a subject Bridget definitely wouldn't
have approved. I didn't either, but I was too tired to object.

The biggest problem was getting Drake to leave. By the time
we'd tucked everyone in for the night, and Sam more than
once, I was ready to go to bed, too.

"Doesn't all this domesticity do something to you? I kinda
like this homebody feeling." Drake put his arm around the
unresisting lump that I had become, sitting on the couch.

"Five more full days of this before I'm set free."

"Now, Ms. Sullivan. Where are your latent motherly im-
pulses?"

"I was born without them." I yawned, hugely, and Drake
couldn't keep his own jaws still.

"It is tiring, isn't it?" He hugged me a little closer. "I was counting on getting a couple of twelve-hour nights of sleep this weekend. Been up late three nights in a row."

"You can get to bed early tonight if you leave now."

He gave me a look. "You're adorable when you're so eager."

I was too tired even to take umbrage. "I'm sure you've figured out that pushing a romantic relationship on someone in the terminal stages of exhaustion would not produce quality results."

"Don't you feel the need of having a man around tonight?" He looked hopeful. "You want some protection, right?"

"I have Barker. He's all the man I could deal with right now." Barker stirred on the floor when he heard his name. He was stretched out on top of our feet, every so often sighing an enormous doggy groan.

"That mutt." Drake stood up, taking his feet away from Barker and his arm away from me. I was, of course, relieved. "Some day, Liz, you are going to stop running so hard. I just hope I'm still around then."

Left alone, Barker and I circled through the house, locking windows and doors and finally ending up in our temporary abode, the master bedroom. It was a nice room, furnished with Bridget's trademark of frugality and ingenuity. Tonight, despite my fatigue, sleeping in that big, fluffy bed where procreation had regularly been accomplished made me feel uncomfortable. I read deeply into *Villette* with Barker snoring on the floor beside the bed for some time before sleep claimed me.

The morning came too quickly. I could have used another couple of hours of unconsciousness, but Mick was an early, and noisy, riser, and a lot of scurrying around went on to get Corky and Sam and him off to school. The carpool Bridget had arranged came by to pick up the older boys. I put Moira in the stroller and walked Mick down to his preschool, where we lingered for a few minutes, awed by the way the teachers managed to function in the chaos.

The walk home was very pleasant. Despite her demanding nature, with only Moira to tend I felt pleasantly carefree. We admired a couple of dogs, discussed the first crunchy leaves from the sycamores in Johnson Park, and waved at Stewart and Doug and their buddies, who were starting to deploy their equipment. When we got to Bridget's driveway, Dinah Blakely was parking her car at the curb.

"Am I the first?" She looked cheerful in her red jacket and black jeans. No khakis this time; I supposed she was only going to supervise, not dig. "It's a beautiful morning, isn't it?"

Agreeing with this, I wheeled the stroller up the front walk and sat on the porch steps to disengage Moira. Dinah put down her bucket of tools, took one edge of the tarp that covered the excavation, and pulled it back with a flourish.

Then she screamed, turning away with her hands to her face to stare at me, while incoherent noises came from her throat.

Leaving Moira in the stroller, I ran over to the edge of the sidewalk. Richard Grolen lay facedown in the dirt. The back of his head was hidden by a heavy, jagged chunk of concrete.

He appeared quite dead.

11

THE screaming upset Moira, but, strapped into her stroller with her back to the commotion, she seemed less in need of help than Dinah Blakely, so I turned back to Dinah.

But even as I wondered whether to slap her or shake her out of her screams, she stopped. Falling to her knees beside Richard, she pulled at the chunk of concrete.

"Um, I wouldn't do that." I stepped forward. "We should leave everything just as we found it. Why don't you go call the police and I'll stay with the body?"

She didn't answer at first, just flung me a disgusted look. With the chunk of concrete off his head, Richard didn't look so bad. True, the back of his head was smashed like a soon-to-be peeled hard-boiled egg. Dinah pressed her fingers into his neck, then turned his face out of the dirt.

"Look," I said, kneeling beside her. "You shouldn't be touching—"

"He's alive, you idiot!" Her words came out sharp and loud. She groped in her handbag, still anchored to her shoulder by its strap. "Forget the police. Call an ambulance." She pulled a compact out of her bag, yanked it open, polished the mirror briefly on her sleeve, then held it near Richard's face. Slowly, almost imperceptibly, it clouded.

I leaped up and raced for the steps. Moira made urgent noises as I went by. "In a minute," I told her, taking the steps two at a time.

My voice choked with hope and dread, I told the 911 dispatcher where to send an ambulance immediately. She wanted me to stay on the line, but I had other calls to make.

I dialed Drake's home number, knowing he probably hadn't left for the day yet. With the phone cord stretched to its utmost, I could see Moira at the foot of the porch steps, her little face screwed up angrily. Beyond her was an incongruous picture: Dinah Blakely using her small archaeologist's brush to whisk the dirt away from Richard's face.

Drake answered on the third ring. "What?" His voice was surly—no coffee yet.

"Come over right now."

"What now? Someone walk off with the dirt this time?"

"No." I looked out the door again. "Someone added something fresh to the display. Richard Grolen."

"Holy shit." Drake hung up, so I did, too.

I grabbed a packet of graham crackers and headed outside. Moira was easily placated with a cracker, but when the sirens started, she wrinkled up her face again.

Unfastening her from the stroller, I hitched her onto my hip, and went over to see what Dinah Blakely was up to.

She paid no attention to me. Her face was set in lines of fierce concentration, despite the tears that leaked down her cheeks. She didn't seem to hear the sirens growing steadily nearer. I stepped into the street when the ambulance turned the corner, waving them to the house.

Then Drake's car horn blared behind me. I jumped out of the way, making Moira laugh.

Drake was talking on his cell phone. He got to Richard Grolen in a dead heat with the emergency medical technicians.

"This one's mine," he yelled, holstering the cell phone. "I'm getting my scene-of-crime team here now."

"The hell he is," said the lead EMT, a tall, muscular black man. "Move it, Drake."

"Look, Smitty—"

"He's still alive, asshole. Now get out of the way."

Drake stepped back, nearly onto my foot. "He's alive?" He turned to me. "Why didn't you say so?"

"You hung up." I watched the EMTs swarming around Richard. Smitty got rid of Dinah by the simple expedient of lifting her up and setting her aside. She perched on the curb, slumping now, all her purpose and determination drained away. "If it wasn't for Dinah, he wouldn't be. I can tell you that much."

Dinah didn't move when she heard her name. Drake narrowed his eyes. "Why don't you tell me about it?" His voice was dangerously low. "I hate being the last to know anything."

"He was under the tarp when she pulled it back. I'd just gotten back from walking Mick to preschool." I shifted Moira to the other hip. She was entranced by the flashing lights on the ambulance. Probably she was being traumatized for life by these experiences—but at least she was alive. I hugged her warm little body closer. "He was lying there. A big chunk of concrete where his head should have been. I thought he was a goner."

"Is that the concrete?" Drake homed in on the fatal chunk. It had been pushed aside. Even as he looked, one of the EMTs stepped on it. Drake, howling a little, whipped off his shabby tweed jacket and dashed into the melee. He emerged with the concrete wrapped in his jacket. "It may be the only piece of evidence available, after these lummoxes get through trampling everything." He sounded bitter.

"Why don't you tell them to be more careful?"

"I don't get in the way of people doing their job." He watched intently, nevertheless, and at the first break in the action he left my side to question Smitty.

"I don't know." Smitty wiped his forehead on the back of a sleeve. "The man's damaged, that's for sure. Looks like no cervical injuries, just the blunt trauma. Crushed the back of his head in. But that wasn't the worst thing. My bet is that in another few minutes, he'd have suffocated." Smitty nodded toward Dinah, who stared blankly back at him. "You shouldn't have moved him, miss. He might have had a neck injury that could lead to paralysis. But I have to say that if you hadn't gotten his nose out of the dirt, he'd likely be dead."

A little of the color came back into her face. She stood up. "I want to go with you. I want to stay with him."

"You his wife? Sister? Daughter?"

Dinah didn't have the presence of mind to lie. Smitty shook his head, watching while the techs loaded Richard into the ambulance. "Then you're not authorized to ride along. You'd just be in the way while we're stabilizing him, anyway." He turned to Drake. "Sorry about your footprints, Sherlock. We had a job to do."

"Yeah, yeah." Drake clapped him briefly on the shoulder. "Go do it, then."

"Okay, then. I'm gone." Smitty swung himself into the ambulance, and it roared away, sirens going, lights flashing. Moira clapped her hands.

Dinah started toward the excavation, maybe to pick up her compact, which had fallen near the place Richard's head had been. Drake held her back. "Let's not mess it up any more." He was watching down the street. More sirens, more flashing lights. This time it was a police van, closely followed by Bruno Morales's Honda. "Took you guys long enough."

"We waited to let the ambulance get out of the way." Bruno glanced at our faces when he vaulted out. "Parking is tight, Paolo. You know that."

I couldn't tell if he was joking or not, but Drake smiled. "They've made a hash out of the ground, Bruno. Maybe you can find something out anyway."

"I'll try." The uniformed officers were hauling stuff out of the van, but Bruno didn't pay any attention to them. He stood at the edge of the excavation, his eyes devouring the ground.

Squatting, he checked it out from every angle. Once he glanced at Dinah's feet and mine. Drake waited patiently.

Finally Bruno shook his head. "Sorry, Paolo. It's been dry, and too many people have trampled around. I can see where she—" he nodded toward Dinah—"knelt beside him. Two hollows for her knees, two dents behind for the toes of her shoes." He indicated the area, and we all nodded solemnly. "But you already knew that. And you probably figured already that judging from the way he fell, he was hit from behind by someone standing in or near the driveway. I don't see anything I could pinpoint as the perp's footprints, though. Too many people have stirred it all up." He reached forward and delicately picked up the compact. Without looking at her, he handed it to Dinah, who accepted it numbly.

"Well, thanks anyway, Bruno." Drake was resigned. "Guess we might as well get started."

"Wait." Bruno was still bent over the churned-up earth of the sidewalk excavation. He picked up a silvery piece of foil, folded over and over to make a tiny square.

Dinah peered at it. "Nelson and his gum," she said, sounding disgusted. "He knows better than to drop anything around an excavation."

"So this is fresh?" Bruno took a plastic evidence bag and some tweezers out of his shirt pocket. He put the foil on top of the bag and unfolded it with the tweezers, manipulating them as delicately as a watch repairer. The foil was empty.

"He was chewing gum yesterday, I noticed." I put in my two cents' worth.

Still using the tweezers, Bruno brought the foil up to his nose and sniffed. "Spearmint." He turned it this way and that. "This doesn't appear damp, which it would be if it had been on the ground all night." He slipped it into the evidence bag, and turned to Dinah. "Does he always fold it like this, into a little square?"

She wrinkled her forehead, impatient. "What does it matter,

84

anyway? Nelson is always chewing gum, I know that much. He'll hear from me if he's littering around an excavation." She turned to Drake. "Do you need me? She was here the whole time." She pointed at me. "I want to get over to the hospital."

"In a moment." Drake's voice was gentle. "You were here this morning when Liz came back from her walk, is that right?"

Dinah sighed, blowing up at her bangs. "I got here about the same time she came walking up." She spoke with exaggerated patience. "It was around eight-fifteen, no later than eight-thirty. I like to get an early start, before the crew comes." She glanced at her watch. "Which they're going to do any moment now."

"We'll take care of them."

"Does this mean our excavation is over?"

"That doesn't matter now." Drake led the conversation back where he wanted it. "You and Liz got here at the same time. How did things look to you? Any different from yesterday when you left?"

Dinah frowned. "I don't remember noticing any difference. I wasn't really thinking about how it looked. I thought about what we were going to accomplish, the best way to do that."

Drake nodded, scrawling on his bits of paper. Bruno had his laptop out on the hood of his Honda.

"How about you, Liz?" Drake turned to me. "Did you notice any difference?"

"All I noticed was how inconvenient it is to have no sidewalk in front of your house when you're pushing a stroller." I shivered a little and held Moira closer. She was on her third graham cracker. I didn't know how long that would hold her. I was also feeling insecure about the whole scene. Granted, Drake was unlikely to peg me as a possible suspect. He would be looking at tying it all in with the bones, and I could have had no hand in that. But murder investigations fill me with angst. Drake teases me by saying I like them. I hate them. I never want to be involved. I don't know why they keep swirling around me like this, like I'm some sort of magnet or catalyst for murder.

Dinah was restive. "Is that all you need to know?"

"I guess that gives us something to go on with." Drake closed his notebook. "You can go for now. I'll be talking with you later. You'll be at the hospital?"

She nodded and sprinted for her car. As soon as she'd driven away, leaving the space at the curb vacant, the police team put up their barricades there, stringing caution tape.

Bruno closed up the laptop. "I'm going to start Rhea going door to door," he said, gesturing at one of the uniformed cops. "Maybe someone saw something out here this morning."

"You think it was this morning?" Drake looked thoughtful. "I noticed his back was damp." He looked at the tarp. Though it had been pulled back for a while, it still glistened with condensation on the underside.

Bruno went to talk to the policewoman, and Drake turned to me. "Let's go inside." He brushed cracker crumbs off Moira's cheek. "I need some coffee. I'll make it," he added, catching my eye. "And then we can put our heads together."

"My head has nothing to contribute," I said. I could see my day evaporating—my luxurious day of just one child to mind. My trip to the library, my watering expedition to my house.

"It won't take long." Drake seemed to read my mind. "We need to see where we are here. It might be safer for you and the kids to go away for a while."

That got through to me. I led the way up the stairs, replacing my useless uneasiness about my own position with something more relevant—the knowledge that someone was targeting Bridget's house for violence. Someone who might move on to Bridget's family soon.

12 _____

DRAKE made me a cup of tea while he was brewing coffee. We sat around the kitchen table, Moira drawing designs in the high chair tray with the grape juice she shook out of her sippy cup. Barker seethed around our legs, sensing turmoil in the air, until I sent him to lie down in the living room.

Drake took a big sip of his coffee and sighed in satisfaction. "Now," he said, setting down the cup. "Tell us everything that happened this morning from the moment you opened your eyes."

I went through the list of what we'd done that morning to get everyone off on time. Bruno nodded; he was familiar with that list, it seemed.

"No unusual noises outside? Barker didn't alert you to anything?" Drake cast a look of disapproval through the door at Barker, who was doing his rug impersonation on the living room floor. "He's no use at all if he won't even let you know when someone's being assaulted outside."

"He woke me up this morning." I tried to remember back that far. "He barked, in fact. Usually he just shoves his cold wet nose into my arm until I get up."

Drake grinned for the first time since he'd arrived at the house. "And do you like that?"

"I don't kiss and tell," I said with dignity. "This morning he barked, and I did hear a door slam. When I let him out, I saw the couple next door heading for the health club. At least I assume it was the health club. They had sweats on, and big duffel bags."

"Then what?"

"I took a shower before the kids got up. Then I was busy." I shrugged. "Sorry."

"I think, Paolo," Bruno said, "that Grolen was assaulted while Liz was walking to the nursery school."

Drake nodded. "You're probably right. It was a stupid time to choose—someone must have seen something at eight in the morning."

Bruno shook his head. "I don't know, Paolo. Neighborhoods like this can be deserted after seven-thirty. Everyone's at work or school or day care."

"Maybe Rhea will turn up a neighborhood busybody," Drake said hopefully.

A dull ache in my fingers made me realize that I had my teacup in a death grip. The picture was a chilling one: a body being planted under the tarp in broad daylight while Moira and Mick and I were walking downtown without a care in the world. What kind of person was so desperate to dispose of Richard Grolen that he—or she—would take the risk of being seen?

Footsteps thudded up the front porch steps, followed by brisk knocking at the door. Bruno gestured me back into my seat. "This will probably be for us to take care of," he said, putting his cup on the table. "You just relax."

Drake craned around in his seat to see the front door. "Press," he said, scowling. "Don't talk to them, Liz. We can't stop them from taking pictures, but don't add fuel to the fire."

"I know that." I ladled a few more Cheerios onto Moira's tray. "Look, I have things to do this morning, places to go—"

"But you don't want to see people, right?" He got up, too, and carried his and Bruno's cups over to the sink. "Let us clear away the press and get stuff straightened out. Then you can go."

I had the feeling that he wanted me out of the way. But that was okay. I didn't want to be there, in the midst of his investigation, dealing with the archaeology students and the press and who knew what else. I wanted to be back in my own house without any rug rats to care for, without any bodies turning up. Failing that, I would take Moira with me to the library.

"Did you find out more about the identity of the bones?" I thought I might be able to slip the question in while Drake was distracted and get an actual answer.

"As a matter of fact, yes." Drake patted me on the shoulder. "Thanks for letting us know what Claudia thought, by the way."

"You don't need to sound so patronizing." I clutched the sponge I'd gotten to wipe Moira's tray, barely keeping myself from wiping it across Drake's smug face. "Don't bother to tell me if you don't want to. I'll find out on my own."

He stopped grinning. "Don't stick your nose in, Liz. It was academic until this morning, but now someone's making fresh bodies. You don't want to end up on their list." He took the sponge out of my hand and pulled me close to him. I could smell the lime scent of his aftershave, and the coffee on his breath. "In fact," he said, his voice rougher, "I'd better spend the night tonight. I don't think it's safe for you to be alone here."

"I'm hardly alone." I let myself rest my cheek against his chest. It felt good to be held—too good. "There's—"

"Barker, I know." His voice rumbled beneath my ear. "That mutt is no good as a watchdog."

"Plus four children."

"All the more reason for me to stay." He pulled away, looking at me. "Deal?"

"You're welcome to the sofa bed, of course."

He shook his head, laughing. "You're a hard case, Liz Sullivan. I can't think why I stick around you."

He let me go, just in time. Bruno came back into the house.

"I've sent them away," he said, raising an eyebrow. I turned away, busying myself at the sink. "The archaeology students came. They seemed very upset when I told them what had happened. Rucker is taking their statements."

"I want to sit in," Drake said, all business, as if that soft interlude had never taken place. "Especially the gum-chewer—Nicholas?"

"Nelson," I said. "Seems like an okay kid, really."

"I'll be the judge of that." Drake bustled past me. "Give us a few minutes before you leave. We'll get the students out of the way. Did you get an update from the hospital?" This was to Bruno.

"Still alive. That's all they'll say." Bruno looked sober. "This is a nasty business, Paolo. I don't like these children being mixed up in it."

"That's okay." Drake was casual—too casual. "I'll spend the night tonight."

"I'll make up the sofa bed for you." I had to say it in front of Bruno. But Drake deserved it. "And we'll even fix you dinner for a change."

"Great." His scowl changed to a pleased smile. "I love it when women cook for me."

"I hope you love it when children cook for you." I ushered them both to the front door. "They're very creative with the seasonings, I've always found."

A little of his pleasure drained away, and I felt ashamed of myself. But I didn't like being pushed into a corner, no matter how cozy, how comfy, it was there.

I went around the house, assembling Moira's needs for the next couple of hours, then changed her diaper for good measure. I could hear activity from the front yard, and the more muted sound of the road crew down the block. Moira was relatively mellow, although she took exception to the washcloth.

The police van was still blocking the drive. I took Moira and the diaper bag out to sit on the porch and wait for them to be done, impatient to be about my business, away from all this turmoil.

13

DRAKE and Bruno were talking to the students as a group. Kathy's expression grew more and more shocked; she began crying, wiping the tears away with both hands. Impassive Hobart even clenched his fists.

Nelson's face glistened with sweat, despite the cool morning breeze. He chewed nervously at the ever-present gum. He had turned his back to the excavation site, but he didn't look at Drake either. He just stared into space, wiping his forehead with a grubby-looking bandanna. Even when Bruno showed him the little baggie with his gum wrapper in it, he didn't say anything. But the way he sweated said a lot.

I picked up Moira and strolled around the yard. Not that I wanted to overhear the conversation, but it was too tantalizing to watch without knowing what was said.

Drake looked from Kathy to the white van. "You came in the van without Dr. Grolen this morning? Why?"

Kathy sniffed and wiped her nose on her bandanna. "He said he'd meet us here. That's all I know."

Unexpectedly, Hobart spoke. "Wanted to get over to the Bay early, get some sailboarding in." He jerked his head up the street, where a sport utility vehicle with a plastic rooftop case was parked. "That's his four-by-four there. He showed me his board. Really primo, top of the line. He gets his equipment free, and money besides, because he patented a sailboard design."

"So he was sailboarding early this morning, before he came here?" Bruno typed that into his computer, then gestured to one of the evidence team members, pointing out Richard's car.

"Did you go with him?" Drake pinned Hobart with a look.

"Me? Nah." Hobart's face gradually lost the animation it had while he was talking about sports. "He didn't invite me."

Nelson wiped his face again, more relaxed with the questions focusing on Hobart. Drake looked at him, but didn't say anything.

After the students drove away, I mentioned Nelson's reaction to Drake.

"Yeah, I noticed." He scrawled something on his disintegrating notepad. "He was not a happy camper, for sure. I'll let him stew a little while, and then go talk to him this afternoon."

"Are your guys just about finished out there? Can I get out of the driveway?"

"They're leaving shortly." He put his hands on my shoulders and looked at me straight on. I could hardly bear to see the concern in his eyes. "Listen, Liz. I want you to take care of yourself today. No sleuthing around, no running risks—"

"I'm going to the main library. Then to the community garden, then to my house. Then I'm picking up Sam and Amanda at kindergarten and dropping Amanda off—"

"You're going to see Melanie?"

"It would be hard to drop off Amanda without seeing her mom." I was struck with a thought. "Does she know about Richard yet?"

"Not unless she's the one who bashed him. But she'll find out soon enough. Bruno's got her on his list of people to interview, although she may find out before he even gets there. That woman's ear covers all of Palo Alto."

I was relieved that I didn't have to be the one to break the news. Melanie showed such a proprietary interest in Richard that it was hard to predict how she'd take his current state.

"So I'll see you at dinnertime if not before." Drake licked his chops. "Mmm. I sure do love a home-cooked meal."

"Yeah, I know. There's a whole freeway from your stomach to your heart."

"You guessed it." He watched the police van drive away, then pulled me close again. I thought he might kiss me, but he left after a slow, heart-stirring hug.

It took me a few minutes to calm down enough to tuck Moira into the Suburban and check that I had everything I needed—the baby stuff, the grocery list, and what I needed for notes at the library. I stopped briefly at my place and nipped into the garage for my bucket of gardening equipment.

The reference librarians were delighted with Moira, and kept bringing her crackers and a selection of books they had squirreled away for junior patrons. I looked up the information I needed for the article I was writing, and then asked for the microfiche of the *Palo Alto Times* for fifteen years ago, plus a couple of years on either side.

Scrolling through, I marveled at how hairstyles and clothing that I had considered the height of chic in my late teens could look not only ridiculous but ugly less than two decades later. The real estate section was a real eye-opener. Houses for sale under $100,000! Certainly there were no bargains like that available now. Hamburger at the Co-op was sixty-nine cents a pound.

Even while I did the tourist thing through the year Melanie had graduated from Stanford, I knew it was futile. Drake and Bruno already had leads on the identity of the skeleton, and anyway the attack on Richard had shoved those old bones onto the back burner. I scanned the front pages for anything about drugs, and the police blotter for anything around Bridget's address, but there was too much data and not much point in trying to absorb it. And I had other things to do before I could pick up the kindergartners.

The community garden is behind the main library. It's a

wonderful space, full of exuberant vegetables, luscious berries, and Bermuda grass which, because the garden is organic, can't be poisoned, only dug out. We all curse the Bermuda grass.

Moira hunkered down in front of the strawberry bed and helped herself while I picked green beans and corn and tomatoes and peppers. I went back and forth between my garden and Bridget's, two down and across the path, with the baby trotting at my heels as if substituting for Barker, who wasn't allowed in the garden and could be heard complaining about that from the car.

I stripped the bloated cucumbers off Bridget's vines, and pulled up as many weeds as I had time for. Moira enjoyed the watering until I accidentally sprinkled her. I placated her with a bag of green beans to carry. She munched one solemnly on the way back to the car. If she hadn't tried to feed half of it to the snail she'd put in her pocket, I wouldn't have known about that slimy hitchhiker for a while. It was obvious Moira wouldn't like to see me do what comes naturally to the snail. Instead of stepping on it, I dumped the dregs of coffee out of Claudia's take-out cup, which was still in the front seat cup holder, punched some holes in the plastic lid with a ballpoint pen, and shoved a little grass in the bottom. Moira was delighted with her new pet. She clutched the cup tightly all the way to the elementary school.

I pulled up in front just as the kindergartners streamed down the sidewalk. Sam and Amanda came out, Amanda holding Sam's hand while he looked as if he weren't participating. They each carried drawings stapled to construction paper that we all admired. I loaded them up and drove to Melanie's.

Amanda rushed ahead of me up the front walk, but Melanie didn't answer the door. It was Maria, her live-in help, who scooped up Amanda and admired her picture. I wondered if Melanie was at the hospital, demanding that Richard Grolen return to consciousness. But I felt relieved, as well, that I wouldn't have to talk to her.

I took Sam and Moira with me to my place, feeling the usual rush of protective pride when I steered the Suburban down the driveway. My little cottage is nothing much, especially by Palo Alto standards, which mandate that old houses either be sensitively restored or knocked down for big new houses. Mine is old and although I've painted it, it's still shabby and in need of a few things, the most significant being a new foundation. The front porch tilts a little one way, the steps tilt the other way. But it's all mine, free and clear, and that makes it perfect as far as I'm concerned. I don't care that the kitchen's last upgrade was sometime in the forties, or that the bathroom's claw-foot tub has rust stains that no amount of cleanser and elbow grease have eliminated.

Best of all is my yard, which I'm turning into a garden a little at a time. Drake, who is buying the house in front of mine, the one that faces the street, has a small front yard and a gravel area behind his house to park his car. The rest of the extra-long lot is mine, from the redwood trees at the back to the rosebushes that border his parking area. I have some lawn, which Barker is gradually outgrowing the need to dig up, and a series of raised beds I've created from scrap lumber gleaned from construction Dumpsters. During the summer I'd sold mixed lettuce and sugar snap peas and nasturtiums and herbs at the farmers' market. A couple of restaurants still wanted all the salad mix I could produce. I didn't make a lot of money, but enough to help pay the water bill and buy seeds and soil amendments.

Sam and Moira chased Barker around the raised beds, shrieking with laughter, while I harvested salad mix and edible flowers for my restaurant customers, clipping the baby greens and tucking the flowers into plastic boxes that I collect and reuse. The nasturtiums and borage flowers glowed like jewels in their clear cases. I love the small, substantial rounds of Tatsoi and the sweet crunch of the Little Gem romaine. After I'd

96

eaten close to a handful, I realized it was lunchtime. The kids realized it at the same time.

I stuck the bags and boxes in the refrigerator and got us all a snack. We sat at the kitchen table, Moira propped up on a dictionary and a thesaurus, and ate yogurt and carrot sticks and sugar snap peas—all I had on hand. Either the kids were hungry or the novelty carried them through. They cleaned their plates.

I washed up the dishes while Sam took Moira on a tour of the kitchen, holding her hand and making up great stories about what was behind each cupboard door. Moira loved it. Although the boys are good with her, they generally regard her as not up to much in the way of fun, and prefer to play among themselves. But when one of them gives her attention, it makes her day. She even talked to Sam, which she hadn't done much for me so far. "More," she urged him after the second story. "Tell more!"

"Okay." Sam opened the third cupboard, where I keep bins of newspapers, cans, and bottles for recycling. "This is where the bones live," he said in sepulchral tones. "When everyone's asleep they get up and dance and have cocoa."

Moira liked the sound of that. "Cocoa." She looked at me. "Peas."

I handed her another pea pod, but she threw it on the floor. "Peas," she said, louder now. "Cocoa! Peas!"

"She wants some cocoa," Sam translated for the child-impaired listener. "Please."

Oh. "We have to go now." I glanced at the clock on the stove. Despite the stove's age, the clock keeps good time. "There's still an errand or two to run. We'll have cocoa when we get home, okay?"

Moira opened her mouth for a first-class howl, then fell silent, staring at the kitchen door. I turned to look.

The man who stood there, if "stood" is the right word to use for a body listing precariously from one side to the other, was known on the street as Old Mackie. He wore an ancient porkpie hat, at least I think that's the name of the headgear with the squashed-down front. Perhaps his had mutated into a porkpie after long usage. His long gray overcoat was ripped in several places, exposing the natty turquoise sport coat beneath it. His hair snarled around his face in gray lovelocks, matching the sparse growth on his face, too long to be called stubble, too intermittent to rate the designation of beard. In fact, his whole face resembled his hat; his chin looked to be planning a meeting with his forehead at some point. As he swayed, he began humming his signature tune, "Mack the Knife." Hence the name.

Sam and Moira stared at him, wide-eyed. Moira might decide at any moment to let loose her cocoa frustration in a howl. I didn't know what to do, but I was in the habit of looking after Old Mackie during the rare occasions he stopped in to visit.

"Hello!" I moved forward, pulling out one of the chairs at the table. "Would you like to sit down? We were just having lunch. Have you had yours?"

Old Mackie appeared to notice the kids for the first time. He smiled, revealing the many gaps between his few teeth. "Hrsh chdbrmm," he said, holding out a hand.

Sam took it reluctantly. "He doesn't talk too good," he observed.

"I believe he said, 'Hello, children.' He doesn't see many kids." I guided Old Mackie into the chair and pushed the bowl of sugar snap peas closer to him. "Help yourself. We're just eating them whole, like this." I demonstrated.

Old Mackie fumbled the first pea down, but then he tucked in with a good will. Sam and Moira watched him as if he were an alien.

"I know." I ushered them to the kitchen door. "Why don't you two take Barker into the living room? There's a book there you could read to Moira."

Sam looked apprehensive. "I don't read too well," he admitted. I hadn't thought of that, but of course he was just in kindergarten. "I know, Moira." He tugged her over to the couch and boosted her up. "I'll just read my hands."

I watched them settle onto the couch. Sam held his hands in front of him, palms together, and then opened them slowly, turning them into a book. He began "reading." Moira sat beside him, entranced.

I was entranced, too, but I had to take care of my visitor. I got him a glass of juice, which he downed, and found some yogurt for him, which he also downed. Old Mackie is one of the people I worry about when I feel guilty over not helping out at the Food Closet like Melanie wants me to. He generally slept under a bush at the creek, except when it was raining or very cold. Then, I suppose, he went to one of the shelters set up around the county. But he didn't like the shelters, because for one thing they wouldn't let you drink, and drink was his reason for living. I knew if I looked out beyond the front porch that his shopping cart would be parked by my steps, with his pillow, the rest of his assortment of hand-me-down coats, the cans and bottles he collected—and probably sometimes stole from our curbside recycling bins. They would be turned in for the deposit, and he would buy booze with the proceeds. Probably he had a bottle of cheap wine wrapped in a brown paper bag in the front of his shopping cart at this moment.

Now, however, he seemed happy enough, munching peas and swilling juice. He pulled up one greasy pant leg to show me that he was wearing the socks I'd given him a few weeks ago during a cold spell. They appeared reasonably clean, and he didn't smell much, so he must have been to the Urban Ministry recently for a shower and use of the washer there.

"Wsh kdz?" Lacking those essential teeth, Old Mackie was hard to understand. I generally could guess what he was saying.

"The kids? Bridget's. I'm baby-sitting for a while." I didn't say how long, or that I was living somewhere else. Old Mackie probably wouldn't break into my house. But some of the other street people might, if Drake weren't home.

Old Mackie nodded thoughtfully. "Shaw nudder buddy."

"Nutter Butters?" I knew they gave out those cookies to blood donors. I couldn't imagine Old Mackie being accepted as a donor, though. "I don't have any here."

He shook his head violently. "No, no." That much I understood. "Nudder boddy. Shyd wulk." He jerked his head toward the street. "Tell kup."

I thought about this one for a while. "Another body." He nodded eagerly. "You saw another body—on the sidewalk?" He nodded again. "Here?"

"No, no." Old Mackie was getting agitated. He pointed in the direction of Bridget's house. "Yer fren." He raised his hand, still with a pea pod clutched in it, and whapped the table. "Ouch!"

I stared at him, the pieces falling together. "You saw—you saw Richard Grolen getting hit on the head this morning? In front of Bridget's house?"

Grinning his toothless grin, Old Mackie nodded happily and held out his cup for more juice.

I filled it up, and resigned myself to half an hour or so spent figuring out just exactly what he'd seen.

14

"**YOU** mean he saw the assault being committed and he didn't do anything?"

"He did do something." I poured another cup of tea for Drake and topped up my own cup. I had called him as soon as I'd gotten home, which wasn't until I'd delivered the greens and flowers to my restaurants. Drake had already yelled at me because I didn't detain old Mackie at my house, but I'd pointed out that I had no phone and that Old Mackie hadn't wanted to stay and talk to the police, much as I'd urged him to.

"What did he do? Mull it over till he could mooch some lunch off you?" Drake doesn't like Old Mackie coming around. The Palo Alto police are not really antagonistic toward the street people, who are mostly harmless sorts. But public sentiment has been building against the constant panhandling that goes on downtown and at every major intersection. The police have been moving people along more. It doesn't help when I point out that Old Mackie doesn't really panhandle. Drake still doesn't like him pushing that shopping cart down our communal driveway.

"He knows you have an attitude, so he doesn't want to talk to you. Anyway, he doesn't see too well and couldn't swear to any of it, and is shrewd enough to figure out that he wouldn't make it on the witness stand. He was doing you a favor, Drake. He could have just forgotten about it."

Drake ran his fingers through his hair, a habit of his that will someday result in baldness, as I tell him. "You aren't giving me lunch," he grumbled. "Which, let me point out, I'm missing to come and take down this cock-and-bull story personally from your lips." He gazed at my lips for a moment. I took a deep breath.

"Stop it, Drake. I just thought you'd want to know. Forgive me if I'm wrong."

He put out a hand to keep me in my chair, and left it on my shoulder, warm and—well, I might as well admit it—tingly. I hated having such cliché-ridden feelings. But having them I was. I inched over in my chair, and the hand fell away.

"You're not wrong." He sighed, and went back to nursing his tea mug. "I guess that helps pinpoint the time. All he can say is, he saw someone hitting, and someone falling?"

"He was going through the recycling bins, I think, though he won't admit that."

Drake nodded. "It's against the law. Stealing from the city. If the recycling center doesn't get those cans and bottles, they won't be able to run the curbside program—"

"I know all that. Old Mackie knows all that. He just feels his need is greater than the city's."

"The city doesn't need a lot of cheap wine, that's for sure."

"Would you stop muttering and let me get on with this?" I looked at Bridget's kitchen clock. I don't wear a watch, and usually I have a pretty good sense of the time. But now that I had children's schedules to deal with, I was discovering that I needed to know a lot more closely than the general hour what time it was. "I have to pick kids up at school this afternoon. And if you're still coming over for dinner, we have to buy groceries." That had been a big miscalculation on my part—not getting the groceries that morning with just Moira in tow. Now I would be at the store with four young Montroses, two of them freshly released from their daily incarcerations. It was enough to make any spinster lady feel faint.

"I'm sorry." Drake settled back in his chair, his untidy notebook open. "Go ahead."

Old Mackie had been pushing his shopping cart up Bridget's street, headed for the creek. He'd been stopping at all the curbside bins, rummaging through them as quietly as he could, keeping an eye out for the truck that picked up the recycling. He hadn't been able to pinpoint the time, also being a nonwatch wearer, but I figured it for around 8:15, a time when most of the worker bees were on their way to their hives, but before the recycling truck came around.

Despite being a little deaf, he'd still heard an altercation behind him across the street, but he hadn't paid much attention. He'd fished out the bottles he wanted, stowed them tenderly in his cart, and looked around to see if the truck was coming. Instead he saw the figures across the street like a tableau shown through gauze—one person turning around, as if to leave, the other stooping for the chunk of concrete and lashing out. He couldn't even say if they were male or female. In the instant after the impact, he'd turned his cart around and headed back the way he'd come, shambling as fast as he could. The assailant might have heard his cart rattling down the sidewalk, but the recycling truck had turned the corner, and it was plenty noisy on its own. Old Mackie had spent a couple of hours crouched in a service alley behind a condo complex before venturing out again. I thought he'd probably be lying low for a while, and not just because he didn't want to talk to the police.

Drake sighed at the end of the story. The house was quiet; Moira was napping and Sam having downtime on his bed, which meant he was probably napping, too. "This doesn't really get me any closer," he said morosely. "The guy wasn't even wearing a watch, for pity's sake."

"You might be able to find out when the recycling truck made its rounds. Maybe the driver saw something. They sit up high in those trucks."

"Teach your grandmother," he said, standing up. "I've got to get back to the office. We have no good leads, but we still have to follow up on all these bad leads. What time is dinner?"

"I don't know. When can you come?"

"After six," he said, giving it some thought. "I might have to go out again later to catch up on the paperwork. But I am staying here tonight. I don't like this happening so close to Bridget's kids. So close to you. Maybe we should tell Bridget and Emery."

"The kids are supervised practically every minute of their day." I didn't want to endanger them either, but I knew Biddy really needed her vacation. "We could all go live at my house, I guess."

Drake heard my lack of enthusiasm. "Guess your place isn't really set up for kids, or big enough either."

"Four carloads of toys would solve the first problem, but nothing solves the second one." I gave him a grateful smile. "You'll find out who's doing this soon. Then I won't have to go."

"Your confidence would be gratifying if it wasn't misplaced," he growled, and left. I spent a few minutes trying to figure out what to make for dinner and what ingredients we'd need. We had beautiful fresh green beans and salad makings, sweet tomatoes and cukes and even some small red onions. We were perilously close to being out of the major Montrose food group, cold cereal, and its accessory, milk. I jotted those things on the list, along with fruit, crackers, and peanut butter, which also were in short supply.

Sam wandered into the kitchen, rubbing his eyes. I asked him what everyone liked.

"Pizza," he said promptly.

"We had that last night."

He looked puzzled. "Noodles," he decided finally.

Noodles it was. Moira woke up a few minutes later. After the usual hectic diapering, juicing, crackering, banana peeling, and assembling the multitude of gear, we stuffed ourselves in the car and drove to the preschool for Mick and to Addison elementary school for Corky and the two other kids in the carpool. The car filled with noise. I plugged in a Raffi tape, only to be ordered by Corky to turn it off. "It's stupid," he said heatedly.

"I like it."

"Me, too," one of the carpool kids said. The other one, the only other girl in the car besides Moira, chimed in. Corky crossed his arms and seethed in silence while Raffi sang about the big beautiful planet. The song had a soothing naïveté that I found refreshing. All of us but Corky sang along.

After we dropped off the carpool kids, I let Corky pick the music to put him in a better mood for grocery shopping. He chose Ray Stevens, not exactly music. I was thankful the drive to the Co-op didn't take too long. We blitzed through the store, leaving a wake of crumbs from the four boxes of animal crackers I bought to ensure compliance. The kids had many suggestions.

"Why can't we just have Spaghetti-Os?"

"I like those Sugar-Marshmallow-Cocoa-Charms cereal!"

"Cocoa—peas!"

"Mom lets us drink Coke. Really!"

I ignored all of them. We did get back home without an actual scene. I made cocoa all around with those instant packets, of which there was a lifetime supply in the pantry. Moira was happy, and I was able to put away the groceries before the next crisis began—cooking dinner.

15 _____

"**HI**, honey, I'm home."

The boys glanced away briefly from "Square One," waved at Drake, and went back to viewing. Moira didn't even look up from the noodles she was picking off her high chair tray.

I turned from the stove and smiled at Drake. "Who are you? Ward Cleaver?"

"I've always had that ambition." He gave me a sitcom-dad kiss on the forehead. "Hi, June."

"Not in front of the children, Ward." I fended off his puckered lips. "You'll get drool in the noodles."

"Noodles? June always had pot roast for her man."

"That was then, this is now." I whacked him with the wooden spoon. "Besides, you're not my man."

"We'll see about that." Before I could respond, he took the spoon out of my hand and stirred the contents of the pot. "This looks like fettucine Alfredo."

I took the spoon back. "Why don't you dress the salad? We're about ready."

"Let me put down my stuff." He disappeared into Bridget and Emery's bedroom—the room I was using—and came back without his shabby tweed jacket and the bulging briefcase that went back and forth to his office with him.

I tipped the fettucine into a bowl, shook the green beans out of their pan, and turned off the oven on the garlic bread. It had been a strain to get so many dishes ready at the same time. I generally have a baked potato or rice along with steamed veggies or a big salad in the evenings. Never wash more than one pot or one dish is my motto.

I stuck my head into the living room to tell the boys that dinner was ready. "Square One" was just ending in a lavish production number. "Nine, nine, nine," sang the perky actors. "That magic number nine."

Drake was putting pieces of cucumber on Moira's tray when I turned back into the kitchen. I started to tell him not to bother, since she wouldn't eat it, but she confounded me by smiling sweetly at Drake and crunching down on a slice.

"You can sit next to her," I said, arranging the garlic bread in a basket. "She likes you."

"She likes you, too," he assured me.

"Really?" I waved a small piece of garlic bread in the air to cool it, then put it on Moira's tray. With a disdainful motion of her small hand, she pushed it off the edge. Barker, who'd already learned to lurk beneath the high chair, snapped it up, crunching with gusto. After this child-tending gig was over, I would have big trouble getting him back on his dog food–only diet.

"You must have alienated her somehow." Drake accepted the seat beside the high chair. The boys surged into their chairs, and I sat at the head of the table with an unaccustomed feeling of hostessy accomplishment.

I didn't sit long, though. Many times when I'd been at the Montrose house for dinner, I'd seen Bridget hop up and circle the table, dishing out food onto her children's plates, and wondered why she didn't just let them wait on themselves. Now I found myself circling the table, coaxing green beans onto Mick's plate, helping Corky handle the salad servers, assuring Sam that I'd grown all the vegetables in the salad, while preventing him from taking a huge mound of noodles and leaving none for Mick. "You can have more later if you want." I wondered if I was channeling Bridget, if she in Hawaii had any idea that I in Palo Alto was parroting her words, her actions, her total mom-schtick.

Drake found it all hilarious. He did his part by overacting his delight in the victuals. The boys shoveled it in with occasional detours into poking each other. Moira sucked noodles slowly into her mouth, reflecting on each one, and rejecting the ones that didn't meet her invisible standard. Drake kept giving her noodles, oblivious to her increasing restiveness, until she cut him off with a businesslike howl.

I took her over to the sink for a quick hose-down and de-bibbing while Drake cleared the rest of the meal. He tried to put his arms around me after depositing the dishes on the drain-board, but I forestalled him by turning and handing him the baby. "She's wet."

"Where's the towel?"

"No." I took the tea towel out of his hand when he started dabbing at Moira's smeary overalls. "Her diaper's wet."

He blanched. "You don't want me to—"

"Why not?" I turned back to the sink and started rinsing dishes. "Use the disposable diapers. There's a stack of them right by the changing table, and one of those step-on trash cans."

"But—but she's a girl baby!"

"So?"

"All the—equipment is different. Everything's—funny."

"You'll manage."

While he was gone—and it took the best part of twenty minutes—I tried to figure out my problem with Drake wanting to be my honey. I was attracted to him physically. He made me downright quivery sometimes. But the closer he tried to get, the more I backed away. My intimate experience of men was limited to my ex-husband, who'd engendered such fear and loathing in me that at one time I tried to kill him, which earned me several years in a correctional facility for women.

Tony's recent death at someone else's hands had freed me, I thought, but inside my head he was still alive, telling me I wasn't worth a man's attention, that I didn't have what it took to satisfy a man. And my own experience told me that love is just a source of pain for a woman.

The kitchen was almost clean by the time Drake came back with Moira. "I put her sleeper on," he said proudly. I didn't mention that he'd put the bottom half on backwards, though the little plastic feet pointing behind her should have been a dead giveaway. "Hey, I would have helped you with the dishes if you'd waited."

"I took care of it."

Moira squirmed to get down, then sat on the floor and tugged on her toes. "Feets bad," she said, her eyebrows puckered. "Bad!"

I pretended not to notice. Drake watched her for a minute before he figured it out. "Just a minute." He scooped her up again. "We'll be right back."

He would make some kids a good father. But they wouldn't be mine. I just don't have it in me to be a mother. I could cope with this temporary version, and I did like Bridget's children and enjoy them for short stints, but the concept of the endless responsibility that parenthood carries is too scary.

The rest of the evening went by in a blur of stories, games, constant picking up of toys, shooing the boys into bed, rocking Moira into somnolence, putting Sam back to bed again. I might have collapsed if Drake hadn't been there. When the kids were finally down and staying, we both sat in the quiet living room for a few minutes, stunned by the silence.

"So I didn't get to ask you this afternoon," I began. I was determined to get some answers to questions that had been nagging me all day. "How's Richard Grolen doing? And exactly what did you find out about the bones?" I felt safe bringing up this topic with the children in bed.

Drake took off his glasses and rubbed his eyes. "Grolen's holding his own. The MRI looks positive, but the docs say he'll be in a coma for a while—maybe days. They expect him to pull through, barring complications. He was found soon after the attack, and that's in his favor."

"And Dinah Blakely? She seemed pretty distraught."

"She was still at the hospital when I checked in there this afternoon." Drake moved a little closer on the sofa, his arm tightening around my shoulders. "Melanie was there, too. Had a bit of a confrontation with Dinah over who got to sit next to Grolen. The ICU staff had to threaten to toss them both out before Melanie would leave."

"Melanie is really acting strange." I tried to ignore the warmth stealing through me at Drake's touch. "What Richard said to her yesterday while I was in the Suburban—like he knew something that she wouldn't want to come out. Do you think—nah. No way she would get so possessive over him if she'd bashed him with that chunk of concrete."

"She sure seems to have a thing for him." Drake sounded absentminded. His hand made little circles on the ball of my shoulder.

"But what about Hugh? Do you think they're having marital troubles?"

"I'm not particularly interested in someone else's relationship right now." He tightened his hand, turning me to face him. Paralyzed by indecision, I couldn't move. His face came closer.

The phone rang.

I jumped up, almost taking out Drake's nose on the way. "The phone!"

"Let it ring." He stood, too, reaching for me.

"It might be Bridget. She'd be worried." I rushed to pick up the receiver, relieved and disappointed at the same time.

It was Bridget, sounding happy and relaxed. "Hi, Liz. Sorry

I didn't call earlier, but we just got back from a surfing expedition. Are the kids in bed?"

They weren't anymore. Corky popped out of his room, Sam behind him. They seethed around, demanding the phone, and I let them each speak to their mom and dad. Then I had to answer Bridget's questions and reassure her that things were going well. The boys said good night, getting a bit choked up in the process, and took twenty minutes after we hung up to settle down again. I was just glad that Mick and Moira had slept through it.

The phone rang again. I glanced apprehensively at the boys' bedroom door, but they stayed down.

"Bruno, for you." I handed Drake the phone.

He listened, hung up. "Bruno wants to get together, review the data. I'm going over to his house." He came closer, putting his hands on my shoulders. "Then I'll come back. I don't want you here alone tonight."

His eyes asked a question.

"I made up the couch." I hesitated, not knowing what else to say. Despite the feelings he created in me, I couldn't offer him a place in Bridget and Emery's bed. I kept imagining Sam getting up in the night, finding us together. "This—is not the seductive hideaway of your dreams, you know."

"I know." He kissed me on the forehead and headed for the door.

"You didn't tell me about the bones. Did you identify them?"

"There's nothing positive yet. I'll tell you more tomorrow." He left, jingling the house key I'd given him. I pulled out the sofa bed and fluffed the pillows, locked up, and took Barker with me into the bedroom. He was the only male of my acquaintance content to sleep on the floor beside my bed, a gallant, if hairy, knight.

I fell asleep quickly, despite my turmoil. I dreamed that

111

someone came into my room, sat on the bed, smoothed my hair back, kissed me warmly. But in the morning I was still alone in the wide expanse of sheets.

16

I got up when I heard sounds from the kitchen, even though the clock said six A.M., far earlier than the kids arose.

Drake sat at the table, drinking coffee. He'd made himself some toast. I started a large pot of oatmeal and got out the jar of Bridget's extra-special blackberry jam from its hiding place. It's not that children shouldn't have jam; Bridget is lavish with the strawberry and plum jams, also homemade. Anything so wonderful as that wild blackberry jam is too fine for their wee, untutored palates.

Drake appreciated it. His heavy frown lightened a little after he spread a liberal amount on the toast.

"What's wrong? Get up on the wrong side of the sofa bed this morning?"

He gave me a Look. "Every side of that bed is wrong."

I regretted even starting that topic. "You don't have to stay here," I said, hating the defensive note in my voice but unable to moderate it. "There's no danger, and if there was, Barker would let me know."

"Huh." Barker had taken up a stance by Drake's knee, seeking and getting head scratches, but Drake stopped petting to glare at me. "You credit this mutt with far too much sense."

"He's got no sense at all, I know that." I stirred the oatmeal. "But he's a deterrent. Kind of like those car alarms that go off all night long."

"And how much attention does anyone pay them?" He chomped on his toast and couldn't help smiling.

"Blackberry jam hath charms to sooth the savage policeman," I murmured, setting a bowl of oatmeal in front of him. "Try this. It's Bert's favorite."

Drake eyed the oatmeal suspiciously. "I don't eat much breakfast, you know that. And who's this Bert?"

I started trying to explain the "Sesame Street" hierarchy, on which I was rapidly becoming an expert, but gave up the notion. "Nobody. And you do, too, eat breakfast. You just go down to Jim's Cafe for it."

Drake evidently thought his frequent forays into bacon-and-eggs territory were a secret. "Who told you that?"

"Seen you there myself." I poured a cup of tea and sat down across from him with my own bowl of oatmeal. "See, this is what domesticity is about. An opportunity to quarrel early in the day."

That got another smile. "What makes you so chipper?"

"The children will all be gone for the day." It was a happy little refrain in my head—the children are gone all day, hey, hey.

"So what will you do with your time?" He leaned across the table. "Let's see how well I know you. You'll go for a swim, work in your garden, do some writing—"

"I've got my workshop at the Senior Center. And some errands. But you're right about the swim, and maybe if there's time, I'll get to all those weeds I saw yesterday."

Drake looked smug. "That's what domesticity is about."

Corky and Sam erupted into the kitchen. "Oh, boy," Sam cried. "Oatmeal! Bert's favorite!"

Drake got up hastily. He's really not big on early morning vivacity, certainly not the brand practiced by the Montrose offspring. "Well, I've got to run. I want to go by the hospital and check on Grolen. And I'm expecting a fax about the dental records today."

I followed him into the living room after helping the boys dish up their breakfast. "Must you leave so soon? Moira will be waking any minute now, and she'll need changing."

Drake made a big show out of folding up the sofa bed. "You make it sound very tempting, but I'm out of here."

"Bye, honey!" I made June Cleaver faces at him until the door shut.

Mick was struggling into his clothes when I looked in the boys' bedroom. I gave him a hand with his shoes and established him at the table with some breakfast. I got Moira up and changed, but knowing her feeding habits, I left her sleeper on. She only cried a little bit. I felt proud.

After a frantic few minutes of wiping jam off faces (I'd forgotten to hide the blackberry, and the boys made great inroads), brushing teeth, and finding school backpacks, Corky and Sam flew out the door when the carpool mom honked.

Melanie came in a few minutes later, while I was still getting Moira's multitudinous equipment ready.

"Don't worry about that," she said impatiently when she saw me stuffing disposable diapers into the bag. "I've got everything at my house. Amanda and Susana are in the car, and I'll take Mick as well and drop him at preschool with Susana." She picked up Moira and cuddled her. I had cleaned her up after breakfast, putting on her grass-green leggings with little white polka-dots and a fleecy green dress that matched. With her red curls brushed and her nose freshly wiped, she looked a picture, and for once she acted as sweet as she looked, returning Melanie's hug and blinking her big blue eyes.

"Thanks, Melanie. I really appreciate this."

"I'll enjoy having a baby to spoil for a while," Melanie said, waving away my thanks. We both knew that her live-in helper, Maria, would pick up the slack for her. Maria was known to dote on babies.

"Have you heard this morning how Richard is?"

Her face tensed. "The hospital won't say anything except

115

that he's doing as well as can be expected. Can you find out more than that from Drake?"

"I'll try. He doesn't always tell me things, but I'll call you if I find out something new. Last night, he said Richard was probably going to pull through."

She swallowed. "Poor Richard. I don't understand what anyone could gain from trying to kill him."

"Maybe he remembered something that was dangerous to someone."

She gave me a sharp look. "I've now told everything I remember to that nice Bruno Morales. I'm sure he'll work hard to find out what's happening."

"I'm sure he will." I didn't tell her that Bruno was involved in another case, and wouldn't be free to devote himself to this one for a couple more days.

She carried Moira out and got her strapped into one of the convenient built-in car seats her luxury minivan came with. I followed with Mick and the diaper bag and toy bag. Moira waved nicely to me—of course, Amanda and Susana, two ruffled little beauties, were waving, too.

The house was quiet. I spent exactly two minutes enjoying it before clipping the leash on Barker and heading for the door.

The excavation site was deserted. All the police seals and fences looked untouched. I wondered what would happen to the first body, now that Richard had horned in on its territory. Maybe the police would just bring over that Bobcat and scoop it all up.

Perhaps that possibility was in Stewart's mind. He jumped down from his truck when he saw me coming and intercepted me. His shambling sidekick, Doug, was with him.

"Say, we heard somebody else was killed here the other day. What's happening, anyway?" Stewart's brow was furrowed with concern. Doug stared, fascinated, at the trench where the sidewalk had been.

I shrugged. "Your guess is as good as mine. Someone was injured—maybe an accident. The police are looking into it."

"Should have let us dig up those bones." Stewart looked back at his crew, who were preparing to lift huge metal plates off the road with a portable crane. The boys would have loved it. He seemed to be on the same wavelength. "Your young ones at home?"

"School today." I yanked back the leash. Barker was getting restive. "I've got a lot of errands to do—"

"Sure. We gotta get back to work, too. Just wondered how it was going." He glanced at the police barricades around the sidewalk and his lip curled. "Mark my words, they'll be asking us to clean it up before this is over."

"You may be right." I watched them walk away. Stewart pulled on a hard hat. Doug, whose hat was already on, had his chin on his shoulder, looking at the scene of the excitement as if he couldn't get enough of it.

Barker set a brisk pace for the two blocks to my house. Drake's car was gone from the parking area that separated his backyard from my front yard. I unlocked my door to get my swimming things together, and then opened up Babe's side door for Barker. Babe is my blue VW bus. She started with a little encouragement. I was happy to be back in the familiar driver's seat, with Barker sitting tall in the passenger seat. After Bridget's Suburban, Babe seemed very brisk and supple, pouring around the corners and whipping into a tight parking spot in front of the tennis courts.

Leaving Barker to guard the car, I walked through the Magic Forest to the pool. The morning lap swim had less than an hour to go, and the pool was relatively deserted. I changed and got a lane to myself.

I don't swim fast or even particularly well. But I love the exercise, the sleek way my body cleaves the water, the breath streaming away from my mouth in silver bubbles. I wanted to think about the whole bewildering problem of the attack on

117

Richard Grolen, but one of the best things about swimming is the inability to think in the usual linear fashion. My thoughts took on the color of the sky, the feathery redwoods stretching up above me as I backstroked for a lap, the intricate branches of an ancient valley oak that filled my vision while I sidestroked.

After my swim, I shower in the locker room. This is a holdover from the days when I lived in Babe with only a tiny sink and cold water for my ablutions. I swam every day, as much for the shower as for the exercise. Now I shower at Rinconada to save my own water. It's not because the shower is pleasant—it's a powerful stinging experience that leaves my skin flayed. But the habits of thrift are the only things standing between me and an ordinary nine-to-five job.

I was fastening my jeans when Emily Pierce spoke to me.

"Liz! I wondered if I'd see you here this morning." She ran a comb vigorously through her short iron-gray curls. "I've finally got something to read this afternoon."

Emily was one of the attendees in the writing workshop I ran at the Senior Center two days a week. It paid a little stipend, and I enjoyed hearing the stories of these people who had so much to tell. Emily had done more listening than reading in the past couple of months, but that was okay, too.

"I look forward to hearing it." I pulled on my T-shirt and made sure I had all the toiletries I'd brought. Replacing those little bottles can be expensive if I leave them behind. I can usually refill them from bigger bottles many times before they wear out.

"I'm dividing my scabiosa," Emily said, stuffing her brush back into a bag. "You want some?"

"Sure." Emily was an avid gardener. More than once she'd helped me with a problem, and she'd been the one to introduce me to the master gardening library at the Gamble House. "Emily, you've lived around here for a long time, haven't you?"

"Since my undergraduate days at Stanford." She walked with me out of the dressing room, and we stood in the sun by the baby pool. "Met my husband there—he was in graduate school after the war. We settled down here. Bought one of the first Eichlers. We moved over here after the kids left—it was smaller and closer to things." She gestured toward the Magic Forest. I knew she lived on one of the streets near the Community Center.

"You must have seen some changes."

"My, yes." She sighed. "It was so rural at first, you know. There were cows pastured on the other side of Middlefield instead of all those houses. Even where the Eichlers were, we were surrounded by fields for years. The children ran wild."

"Your kids—did they go to Stanford, too? Were they part of that whole hippie scene?"

Emily tilted her head. "Are you collecting information for an article, Liz?"

"I'm doing a little preliminary research."

"I liked the one you did for *Smithsonian* on Mayfield. Are you doing Palo Alto through the ages?" She didn't wait for me to answer. "The sixties and seventies are of interest to everyone now, aren't they? Really, although there seemed to be a lot of turmoil at the time, it was pretty benign down here. The real revolutionary action was in Berkeley." She started walking toward the gate, and I kept pace with her. "Of course, that's where my son wanted to go, just to mingle with the other radicals. But he transferred to Stanford his junior year. Not that he said so, but I think some of that rhetoric kind of scared him."

"Did he live with you?"

"Heavens, no." She laughed. "He wouldn't have been caught dead living with us. He had a room in a group house over on Palo Alto Avenue. If you want the truth, I think his girlfriend shared the room with him. But we adopted a 'don't ask' policy long before the military did. They showed up at our house for dinner on Sundays, and we made the washing machine available if they should want it. Despite the way they looked, they were pretty clean."

"You have a daughter, too, right?" We stopped beside Babe.

"Oh, yes. My daughter actually went to Vassar. She was much more conservative—then." Emily laughed. "Now she's the environmental activist, and my son has turned into a very button-down insurance broker. You never can tell."

"Would he be willing to tell me any stories about his college days? Or has he put that behind him?"

She looked thoughtful. "I'll give him a call when I get home. Let you know this afternoon."

I pushed Barker's head back through the open passenger window. "You want a ride home?"

Emily shook her head. "No, the walk is part of my work-out." She strode off down the sidewalk, plump and gray-haired, but in good shape for a seventy-year-old woman.

I didn't know if Drake would think I was meddling or not. But Emily had given me an idea. If I found Palo Alto in the seventies interesting, others might too. Maybe I would do an article on that time, using the bones as a framework.

Then I remembered Richard Grolen. I kept forgetting that he was hovering between life and death over those very same bones. My writer's instinct told me that just made the story more dramatic. But the rest of me found that stance a bit repellent.

I explained it all to Barker on the way home. But he couldn't help me with my moral dilemma.

17 _____

I pulled Babe into my driveway, and immediately felt uneasy. Something was wrong. Everything looked just as usual: The door to the house was closed, the yard empty. I looked at Barker. He didn't have his fur up.

Then I noticed that the garage door was no longer locked.

My garage is old, with two heavy doors that swing out if you exert enough force. I padlock it, of course, but the screws holding the hasp onto the wood had simply been unscrewed, leaving the expensive padlock dangling. The doors had been pushed back together, but they are warped and don't stay shut unless they're locked. Though the gap between them was only six inches of darkness, it raised the hair on the back of my neck.

I sat there for a minute, wondering what to do. Nothing happened, except that Barker grew restive. Finally I opened the door and climbed down from Babe. Drake would have said I should go straight to Bridget's and call from there. But I couldn't leave my territory undefended like that. And if nobody opened fire on me while I sat in my car, I figured whoever had broken in was long gone.

Barker brushed past me. I called him back, but he was busy at the garage door, sniffing with deep interest. His fur stood up a little, but he didn't growl. Another sign that the intruder was gone.

I got the flashlight out of the glove compartment and found

the key to the side door of the garage on my key ring. With Barker at my heels, I approached the door cautiously. It looked untouched. Perhaps its deadbolt had discouraged the intruder.

I put the key in the lock, then turned it quickly and flung the door open. The flashlight switch was stiff; I should have turned it on first. I thumbed it madly and finally it threw a beam of light into the gloomy interior of the garage.

Something unfamiliar, big and bulky, dark and glittering at the same time, confronted me. My heart leaped into my throat. Growling, Barker moved past me, his hackles at their full extent.

The light switch on the wall eluded my groping fingers for a long moment. When I finally switched it on, the dangling bulb in the center of the garage didn't do much to penetrate the gloom. But it did show me the object that had frightened me in greater detail.

Old Mackie's shopping cart.

I recognized it from the neatly folded coats in the front and the big plastic bags crammed with cans and bottles. Barker circled it warily, then came trotting back to me.

I shoved the big doors open, flooding the inside of the garage with light. There was my workbench, with the tools I use to maintain my bus hanging on the Peg-Board behind, and the floor beneath it crowded with paint cans. There were my garden tools, acquired from garage sales and reconditioned with a file, and a bucket of sand mixed with used motor oil, neatly ranged along the wall. Nothing had disturbed the bags of vermiculite and rock dust and chicken manure. The stacks of plastic and terra-cotta flowerpots were still upright.

Best of all, no body. The vision of Old Mackie crumpled into a corner dissipated.

Like Barker, I walked around the shopping cart, careful to touch nothing. Old Mackie's things looked intact. His pillow was in its usual spot, its flowered case grimy.

It took me awhile to realize what was missing. There was no

bottle right in front, wrapped in a paper bag, ready to be uncapped for a swig.

Barker and I checked behind the garage, then around the house. The locks were undisturbed on the front door and on the side door leading to the porch that houses the washer and water heater. Nothing in the yard was out of place, nothing different from the morning. All the little seedlings were still reaching for the sky. Feeling just a tad ridiculous, I stirred the compost piles with the pitchfork. Nothing.

With Barker at my side, and a distinct feeling of anticlimax, I entered the house. Everything was just as I'd left it that morning, down to the half-open drawer in the bedroom that I hadn't closed after yanking out my swimsuit. No bodies in the bathtub. Nothing under the bed but a few escapees from the dust mop. Nothing in the washer, and precious little in the fridge. My computer and all the piles of manuscript, the most important things in the house, were intact.

I got the key to Drake's place from the hook beside the door and went to use his phone. I don't have a phone, partly for reasons of economy, and partly for the same reason I don't have a TV. Reading has always been adventure enough for me.

Drake wasn't in when I called him, of course. I left a message on his voice mail and then tried Bruno's number.

"Morales." He sounded unusually preoccupied.

"Bruno, this is Liz. I'm trying to find Drake."

"He's out interviewing." Bruno sounded guarded. "Is this about the Groler case?"

"I don't know." I sat down in one of Drake's kitchen chairs, after moving a stack of books, papers, and magazines. Most of Drake's house consists of overflowing piles of stuff—predominantly clothes and books in the bedroom, videotapes and books in the living room, newspapers and books in the dining nook of the kitchen. But the cooking half of the kitchen is a scene of rigid order. Not a tool out of place, not a dish left in the sink. His stove-top was spotless. Even the front of the refrigerator gleamed under the rotating gallery of cartoons he'd clipped from various sources.

"Has something happened?" Bruno's voice sharpened. "The children?"

"As far as I know, the children are fine." I glanced at Drake's clock. Already ten-thirty. My precious day was evaporating. "Did he tell you about Old Mackie's visit yesterday?"

"The vagrant. Yes, he told me last night. We have been looking for your friend to verify his statement, but so far we haven't found him."

That didn't sound good. "Well, his shopping cart has turned up in my garage."

Bruno didn't speak for a minute. "Are you in Paolo's house?" He didn't wait for my mumbled yes. "Lock the doors. I'll be right there."

He hung up, and so did I. There went the rest of my morning.

"What did you touch?" Bruno stood beside me, watching the evidence team go over my garage.

"I unlocked the side door and pushed it open. I pushed the big doors open from the inside. That's all."

Bruno nodded. The outside of the double doors had already been dusted, or smoked, or whatever it was they did.

"Where's Drake, anyway?"

"He was looking for your friend." Bruno nodded at the shopping cart. Spotlights illuminated it, as if it were some kind of funky stage decor. The evidence guys hovered over it, delicately testing this and that. I felt guilty when they heaved the bags of bottles out of the cart and began going through them. Old Mackie wouldn't thank me for drawing so much attention to his livelihood. If he were in any condition to complain.

"Why do you think the cart is here?' Bruno propped his laptop open on the trash can at the side of the garage. The evidence team had already checked that it was empty; I hadn't thrown anything away since the previous day, when PASCO had been around to collect the garbage.

"I don't know. But Old Mackie might have parked it here if he was going to drop out of sight for a while."

"Why would he feel he needed to drop out of sight?" Bruno clacked busily at his keyboard, taking down everything I said.

"Probably because he knew I'd tell Drake what he saw, and Drake would buzz around stirring people up, and he didn't want to be at risk." I shivered, though the sun was warm. "I can't imagine him without his shopping cart. Leaving his pillow behind—"

"And his spare coats." Bruno frowned. "What does that suggest?"

"That he won't need them where he's going." The words sounded grim, and I added quickly, "He did take his bottle. Or else he emptied it before he left."

"If he's the one who left the cart here." Bruno studied the driveway. "No way to get any tracks from this dry gravel," he muttered.

One of the evidence guys came up, peeling off latex gloves. "We didn't find anything in the cart but old bottles and cans and some clothes. Nothing in the pockets but a very used hand-kerchief. Prints on the cart's handle match those we could get from the bottles and stuff. No blood, nothing particularly sinister."

Bruno entered this information into his laptop. "Thanks, Dwayne. Guess you guys can go now."

Dwayne nodded and went back to his partner. They started packing up all their equipment—more bulk than Old Mackie's cart contained. I noticed that Dwayne put all the bottles back in their ratty plastic bag. They left the cart looking much the same.

"So what are you going to do?"

"Nothing." Bruno shut his laptop and turned to me. "There's no evidence a crime was committed, and nothing that points to the shopping cart as significant if there had been a crime. More than likely, your explanation is correct—your friend is staying at the Carver Arms or some similar place, waiting for this to blow over."

"Will you keep looking for him?" I wrapped my arms around myself, feeling chilled, though the sun was hot. "What if that puts him in danger?"

"We will be low-key." Bruno patted my shoulder. "You understand that we cannot ignore this occurrence. It fits somewhere into the continuum of these incidents."

"Do you include the first skeleton in your list of incidents, or just Richard's bashed head?"

"We are investigating many things," he said primly. "I am not at liberty to fill you in on them all. But, Liz—" He looked at me, a worried frown creasing his smooth forehead. "You take care, and take care of those children. These activities seem targeted toward the area around Bridget's house. Will Paolo be staying there again tonight?"

"That's up to him." My turn to be prim. "I feel we are perfectly safe with Barker, but we can come over here if it would be better."

"It would not necessarily be better now," Bruno said patiently. "You see, if your friend didn't put his cart in your garage, someone else did. Someone who knows you are involved, and where you live."

This was not a comforting statement. I chewed on it while Bruno put the computer back in its case. "I will advise Paolo to stay with you nights until we clear this up," he said finally, and grinned at me. "It will not be a hardship for him, I think. And you must take care." He held up a hand. "I know you are used to looking after yourself. In this instance, be even more careful." He bent to rumple Barker's ears. "Keep this dog with you."

"Okay, I get the picture." I watched him drive away and felt a bit forlorn, going about locking things up. I screwed the hasp back into the garage door and imprisoned old Mackie's cart, now put back together as it had been left. Too bad if he wanted it and couldn't get at it. I locked the house, too, after rinsing my swim stuff and hanging it in the side porch to dry. Barker and I piled into the bus. I felt safer there than walking. I headed to Bridget's for a quick bite before my class, since my cupboard was bare.

Turning the corner onto her street, I realized I wasn't going to get anything to eat at Bridget's. The fluttering yellow caution tape that festooned the chain-link fence around the scene of the latest bashing was nearly obscured by a crowd of people. Many of them carried big press cameras. Bulky vans with satellite dishes on the roof were parked up and down the street. The media was in hot pursuit of the gruesome news. Drake was there, too, his hair wild, hanging behind the uniforms that strove to create order. Every so often one of the press pack would break free and run up to him, pelting him with questions that he answered with one or two words at the most. He caught my eye as I cruised by slowly, and the tiny motion of his head indicated, "Out of here!" I was only too glad to comply.

I still had to inch past the Public Works guys, though. Stewart was obviously very interested in what was going on in front of Bridget's, but he still waved the backhoes and crane operators into line, between peeks over his shoulder at the media circus.

Doug, however, stood at the edge of the construction, staring at the milling crowd around the crime scene. His face was unguarded, and his expression caught my attention. His mouth was open, his forehead furrowed. The look in his eyes was a compound of anguish and uncertainty.

That look stayed with me all the way down the street. I found a parking place out of the two-hour limit, since I still had to conduct my writing workshop at the Senior Center. I ate a package of peanut-butter crackers from Babe's emergency kit.

It was the last package. Time to restock the kit with the perishable items such as chocolate bars and crackers, perishable because I raid them shamelessly.

And I tried to dismiss that image of the big, shambling man, his distress written all over the face he couldn't mask as normal people do. Certainly he wouldn't lack the strength to heave up that chunk of concrete and bash in Richard Grolen's head.

I just couldn't figure out any reason for him to do it.

18

"**AND** that was when," Carlotta Houseman read in a voice quavering with emotion, "I realized that my beloved home would henceforth be occupied by strangers. That I would go to my grave without ever again tending the beloved camellias planted so many years ago by my dear, departed husband."

She sniffed and laid down the pages of her manuscript. Around the table, we waited a moment, giving her time to dab at her watery eyes and, at least on my part, making sure she was done.

"Well," Janet Aronson trumpeted before anyone else could speak. "I don't think much of your choice of subject matter, Carlotta."

I frowned at Janet. This is not the kind of critique we usually indulge in during the writing seminar I conduct for seniors at the Palo Alto Senior Center two days a week. We are supportive of each others' writing, especially when, as in Carlotta's case, it was autobiographical, with no commercial application in mind.

But several other members of the class were nodding their heads in agreement. "It was tacky, to say the least," Helen Petrie said, sitting back in her chair once she'd delivered that uncharacteristically strong statement. "And didn't you tell us before that you couldn't wait to cash in your house and move to the Forum? I'm sure you did."

"What's the point in bringing all that up again?" Emily

129

Pierce glared at Carlotta. "We're not interested in your fake emotions. Dragging in poor Vivien's death, and Eunice's, too, and implicating Liz—"

Freda Vaughn, another veteran of the class, was filling in a couple of the new members in a penetrating whisper. "Shocking murder . . . poor Vivien . . . Liz inherited . . ."

"Ladies. Let's not get personal." I tried to take control of the situation. "Carlotta is at liberty to choose her subject matter, as you all are. Let's try responding to the merits of the piece. Pretend it's fiction for a minute."

"It might as well be, with so little relationship to the truth." Janet was not to be quenched. She turned to Carlotta, who sat, plump and defensive, at the end of the long conference table opposite me. We were a larger group this fall, which had made me happy. I am paid a small but welcome sum to run the class, and the fewer members there are, the more I worry that it will be canceled. Along with the five returnees—perhaps Carlotta would call them survivors—I had five new members, and had been feeling pretty good about the class for the first few sessions.

Now Carlotta had chosen to write about selling her house to move to a retirement home. This in itself would be nothing extraordinary, but the circumstances around the house sale last fall had been spectacular, to say the least. Two of her neighbors, elderly women who were also members of our class, had ended up dead. And from one of them I had inherited a house with a rental cottage in back, which had for a while ranked me as a suspect with the police. The fact that one of those policemen now lived in front of me, buying Vivien's house while I lived in the cottage, had gone a long way, I thought, toward my rehabilitation in the eyes of society.

But not all of society. Carlotta had never forgiven me for refusing to sell my unexpected inheritance to the developer who was trying to acquire several properties in the neighborhood for a condo complex. She had finally sold her house, and, rumor had it, for a hefty price; certainly she'd ended up at the Forum, a not-inexpensive senior enclave in the hills west of Cupertino.

Now she had turned up again, after skipping the spring session. She'd made a few snippy little comments during the first couple of classes. Her first contribution to the class was the piece she'd just read, where her removal from her home was portrayed as being prompted by the violence, and the subsequent decline in personal safety she felt living there.

And if those other sweet ladies hadn't taken such strong exception to her work, none of the new writers would have known anything about it, so vague were Carlotta's accusations and so feeble her writing skills. As it was, because they'd championed me, she'd created a disruption. Probably just as she'd planned.

"I'd like everyone's attention, please." I rapped on the table, stilling the tumult that had arisen. "We are here to read our manuscripts and offer thoughtful, sensitive critiques to the manuscripts of others. Not to question their motives. Not to create a disturbance." I looked directly at Carlotta, and she looked away, a tiny smile visible for an instant beneath her aggrieved expression. "I suggest we get on with the business of the class. Afterward, I'll stay for a few minutes, and anyone who wants to vent can do it then." I paged through my notes. "Now. Carlotta, I noticed a lot of repetition in your first few paragraphs. You used the words 'dearest,' 'darling,' and 'precious' at least twice each on the first page of your piece. You also used passive voice throughout—'It was then that I was made aware of' instead of the more straightforward 'I noticed.' Sentences beginning with 'It was' or 'There was' are weak; try rewording them to be more active, to engage the reader head-on. Your descriptions were good, but I got kind of lost in a couple of them. I think they might be more effective if you tightened them up."

"Yes," chimed in Pam Cardeñas, one of the new members.

"I couldn't figure out in one place whether you were talking about an actual camellia or using it as a metaphor for your life."

Nods of agreement around the table. "Also," added Freda Vaughn, who was the grammar eagle of the group, "you misused 'lie' and 'lay' again."

Carlotta pouted. "Nobody cares about that stuff," she protested. "I'm only writing for myself. I don't expect to get published, like some people." She slanted a look at Janet, who sent out manuscripts regularly to a cornucopia of magazines, and got most of them back just as regularly.

Janet wasn't safe to pick on. "If you don't want to improve your writing, you don't belong in this class," she growled, taking the thought right out of my head.

"Does anyone else have comments on Carlotta's manuscript?" I glanced around the table. "Okay, let's hear from Emily now. I know she's got something special for us."

Emily blushed. "Well, that's nice of you to say. I'm glad just to have finished a story."

Emily's story was about an idealistic young woman and her parents, who welcome the girl's new friend into their circle, only to become increasingly disturbed by her controlling ways. When she finally leaves, taking with her credit cards, small family treasures, and their trust, the girl who'd befriended her is devastated.

It was a powerful story, simply told, and after Emily finished reading it we were all silent for a while.

"That was good," Janet said, unflatteringly surprised. "You should read more often, Emily."

"I should write more often." Emily pushed back her gray curls. "Okay, let me have it. What's wrong?"

"I only noticed a couple of places where I thought you could tighten it up." I gave her my critique, such as it was. "But I agree with Janet. It's very good."

The other women around the table nodded. A couple offered comments. Carlotta wisely said nothing.

"What are your plans for it?" I turned in my notebook to the listing of magazines I kept on hand. "Are you going to send it out?"

"You think I should?" Emily was hesitant.

"It's worthy of publication, in my opinion." I grinned at her. "That doesn't mean editors will agree with me, but you should give them the chance."

We talked about markets for a minute, then went on to the next manuscript.

Despite Carlotta's disruption, we managed to get through all but one manuscript before the time was up. I had enjoyed the class as a welcome respite, but now I would have to face several unpleasant things. First, talking to Carlotta, the least of my rotten duties. Then, picking up my four charges at Melanie's house—back into bondage. And then, coping with that crowd of people I had seen around Bridget's house when I'd driven by earlier. I wondered if Drake would get rid of them before I took the kids home.

Janet and Emily lingered after everyone else was gone, and they kept Carlotta from slinking out, too. She was puffy with a combination of outrage and uncertainty. I wondered why she had to give me so much grief.

"Do you really want to take this class, Carlotta?"

She tossed her bright hennaed curls. "It's a free country. This class is open to seniors, and I'm sure you don't want me to complain to the Senior Center."

"Actually," Emily said, her gentle voice for once overriding Janet's bluster, "it's open first to residents of Palo Alto. You're not a resident anymore, dear. What are you now—Cupertino? Los Altos? Perhaps you should see if they offer the kind of memoir-writing class you seem to be interested in."

Carlotta was speechless for a minute. "That's a good idea," I said. "You are welcome to take this class if you want to, Carlotta. But you know one of our rules is no personal attacks. I felt personally attacked. I didn't like it."

"So what will you do? Murder me?" Carlotta got to her feet, clutching the marbled covers of her portfolio to her ample bosom. "Wait till I tell the management you're threatening me! You won't be lording it around here very much longer."

She swept out, pushing Janet out of the way.

"Bitch." Janet picked up her own manuscript folder and followed Carlotta.

Emily laid a hand on my arm when I would have gone after them. "Don't worry about it, Liz." She smiled placidly and gathered up her story. "I do volunteer work in the office here, you know. This isn't a private club, where people like Carlotta could have a lot of influence. They'll know exactly how to deal with her. After all, as I told her, she's not even a Palo Alto resident any longer." She looked through her papers and selected one, handing it to me. "I spoke to my son. He said he'd be delighted to reminisce about the old days." She gave me a sharp look. "This wouldn't have anything to do with those bones they found under the sidewalk, would it? I saw something about it in the *Palo Alto Daily News*. Are you investigating that?"

"I don't investigate." I hesitated. "But the bones were found not far from my house, and I'm—interested. Once it's cleared up, the story might make a good frame for an article about Palo Alto in the days of peace and love."

Emily nodded, satisfied. "I thought it might be something like that. Well, that's my son's number. He'll be at home tonight. He said he didn't want to have his name used in any article, but you were free to quote him as an anonymous source." She smiled. "He'd get a charge out of that."

"Thanks, Emily." I tucked the phone number away. "And you wrote a very good story. Very polished."

She shook her head in bemusement. "It just poured out, like it had been in me, waiting for me to tap it. I did know a family who had something similar happen to them. The outcome wasn't the same, though."

"Maybe that's what fiction is, taking the ordinary to extremes." I swung my knapsack to my shoulder. "I wouldn't know. I'm stuck in nonfiction."

"You should try a story or two some time." Emily preceded me out the door, turning to smile. "It might just, as they said in the sixties, blow your mind."

The way my mind was feeling, that was the last thing I needed. "I'll stick to magazines for the present," I told Emily. "Make sure you send that story out, now."

"I will." She patted me on the shoulder. "And don't you worry about Carlotta. She probably just won't ever come back."

I looked past Emily and saw Carlotta marching through the lobby below us. She gave me a thin, triumphant smile. Behind her, Janet Aronson looked worried. "I wouldn't be too sure of that."

Emily hurried down the stairs. "Janet. What happened?"

"I don't know." Janet gave me an apologetic smile. "When I got down there, Carlotta was in the director's office with the door closed, and the secretary wouldn't let me go in. Then she came out and the director rushed off to a meeting or something." She squared her shoulders. "But don't you worry, Liz. I'm writing a letter as soon as I get home, and so will everyone else in the class. We won't let her put something over on you."

Emily echoed this, but she, too, seemed worried. They both walked me out to Babe, and made much of Barker, who'd been having a snooze on the backseat—he regards the bus, as I do, as his traveling living room. I could tell, however, that my friends were afraid that Carlotta was indeed capable of wrecking this small portion of my livelihood.

I gave them both a smile when I left. But I couldn't help being concerned. Why did Carlotta even care? Was this her petty revenge because I wouldn't agree to let my house— Vivien's house—be included in a developer's parcel last fall? It wouldn't break me not to have the workshop anymore, although that little income was one of the components of my meager budget. Far more disturbing, to me anyway, was the notion that anyone disliked me enough to actively work against me.

At any rate, I didn't have time to brood about it. In half an hour I had to retrieve my young charges and become a surrogate mom again. This was a much more troubling thought than dealing with Carlotta's spite.

19_____

THE plan was that I would pick up Corky from elementary school and Mick and Susana from nursery school, and bring them to Melanie's to exchange Susana for Sam, whom Melanie would pick up after kindergarten with Amanda, and Moira. These convoluted battle schemes are common to parents all over the country, who plan and execute much more complicated maneuvers than this every day. I have the utmost respect for them. They must have more synapses, superior ones to mine, to be able to comprehend the incredible nuances of meshing several kids' schedules. Pitchforked into this whirl of carpools and reciprocal pick-ups, I was barely coping.

I did understand, however, that to haul all these kids around legally, I would need Bridget's Suburban, with its fleet of children's car seats. I dreaded having to extract the Suburban from the driveway in the face of that crowd of photographers and reporters.

Parking Babe down the block, I snapped the leash on Barker and led him up the other side of the street for a reconnoiter. We walked quickly past the thunderous din of the Public Works crew. Using backhoes to chew a narrow trench in the road, they were halfway across the street, about two houses down from Bridget's. A noisy cluster of machines hovered over the trench, mechanical surgeons operating on an asphalt incision.

Doug occupied the driver's seat of one backhoe, and Stewart talked busily into his cell phone, making notes on a clipboard. Barker and I went by as inconspicuously as possible. I didn't want to get involved in a conversation with either of them; Doug's unguarded expression earlier that afternoon still haunted me. I wondered if Drake had noticed, if he'd spoken to the man. If I had to work amid such grinding noise, despite wearing ear protection, I might be homicidal.

As soon as we were past all the equipment, I could see that the media circus in front of Bridget's house had vanished. The seething mass of reporters and photographers was gone, leaving not even a solitary TV news truck behind. The relief of avoiding that gauntlet was considerable. I slowed my pace, savoring the crisp, warm air, the ineffable tang of fall. Even the clashing backhoes couldn't destroy the beauty of the day.

I was admiring the rusty red pomegranates on the tree in Bridget's front yard when I noticed something moving behind the chain-link fence at the excavation site. A figure on its hands and knees had folded back the tarp and was quietly doing something in the dirt there. I couldn't make out who it was until the figure straightened and the sun glinted on glasses and shaggy dark hair.

Nelson. He glanced furtively up and down the street, but he didn't notice me on the other side.

Ready to give him a piece of my mind, I began to lead Barker across the street. A car careened around the corner, and I jumped back on the curb.

The car pulled up in front of Bridget's with a screech of brakes, running over some of the caution tape in the process. Nelson clambered to his feet, shoving his glasses up on his nose. Dinah Blakely jumped out of the car.

"What the hell do you think you're doing?" She bellowed really well for such a ladylike woman.

Nelson shuffled his feet. I couldn't hear his reply over the construction noise. Curious, I took Barker a little way farther up the sidewalk and then crossed the street to come up behind the contestants.

Dinah was busy tearing a strip off Nelson. "You're not authorized to come here alone and mess up the dig. I saw your stupid gum wrapper. I know you've been careless. Don't you even have the basics of excavation down? We don't leave so much as a speck of our debris in the dig, not even a hair—"

"Not even a dead body?" Nelson's voice was soft, but now I could hear it. He was fidgeting, but he didn't look particularly cowed.

Dinah stopped in mid-tirade. I couldn't see her face, but her shoulders were held rigidly. "What dead body? There hasn't been a dead body here for at least fifteen years by my reckoning."

"Dr. Grolen was almost dead." Nelson smiled. It wasn't a particularly nice smile. "If you hadn't come along, he would have been dead in twenty minutes. I heard the detectives say so. What happened? Did you change your mind?"

Dinah shook her head, slowly. "You're nuts," she said with conviction. "Implying that—just nuts."

Nelson looked past her, seeing me. His face changed, became meek again. "Oh, hello, Ms.—Um." He shrugged. "We were just—just—"

Dinah swung around. "Oh, it's you." Her tone was dismissive.

"How is Dr. Grolen today? I haven't heard."

Dinah's face closed. "He's still unconscious." Her hands clenched. "If I ever find out who did that to him—" She turned back to Nelson. "Was it you, you little creep?"

Nelson blinked, but the accusation didn't seem to faze him. "Why would I conk him over the head? I had nothing to gain." He glanced at her, his expression sly. "Not like some people. With a department chair in the balance—"

"You—you wretched—" Dinah no longer looked like the proper young woman. With her lips curled back in a snarl she more closely resembled a harpy than a preppy.

Barker didn't like it. He growled, his fur bristling. I yanked the leash and spoke to him sharply, and Dinah seemed to come back to herself. She stepped away from Nelson.

"You are off the crew as of now," she said frostily. "And I'm removing you from the lab. If I were you, I'd think seriously about transferring into another discipline—or another university."

Nelson didn't look too worried. "I'm Dr. Grolen's student, not yours," he pointed out. "He's my advisor."

"All his students have been transferred to me for the time being." Dinah sounded triumphant. "And I'm taking over his lab class as well. He won't be back in the classroom until next quarter, if then." A shadow crossed her face.

Nelson took off his glasses to clean them on his grubby shirttail. Both of them seemed to have forgotten me, and I found their conversation too interesting to interrupt.

"So you've gotten what you wanted," he said, his eyes no longer vague without the glasses masking them. "You've stepped into his shoes, and you're in line for that chair if he should take a while recovering. Or maybe he won't recover. Maybe he'll have a relapse—"

Dinah stepped toward him again. "I'm tired of your insinuations, jerk. Get out of here!"

"This isn't your private domain, Dr. Blakely. I have just as much right to be here as you do."

Both of them remembered me then, turning like a vaudeville team to face me, ready to claim their positions on the site. I held up my hand, the power of the moment going to my head.

"I imagine the police wouldn't see any reason for either of you to be here, especially if you're interfering with their crime scene." I nodded to the chain-link fence, pried open by Nelson, the laid-back tarp. "What were you doing, anyway?"

He put his glasses on and backed a little way toward the curb, a wary eye on Dinah Blakely's angry face. "I was just— checking a theory." Before our eyes, he turned back into the diffident student. "I'll go now."

"What theory?" Dinah yelled the question at him, but Nelson didn't seem to hear. He pulled a bike out of the shrubbery on the far side of the excavation and pedaled off, his pudgy legs really moving.

"He's too much of an idiot to have a theory," Dinah muttered, going toward the fence.

I stepped in front of her. "Good idea. Let's just fasten this up again, shall we? I'll let Drake know, and he'll probably post an officer here so it doesn't happen again."

Dinah threw me a disgruntled look. "I should just—"

"Best to leave it." I pulled the gap in the fence together and turned to face her. "The police know how they left it this morning. If something's different now, it's on Nelson's head, not yours."

Dinah looked thoughtful. "That's true." She hugged her elbows, tapping her fingers impatiently on her arms. "This is all a horror show. Why should that mouthy little jerk be here, messing around? Why should Richard be damaged like this? I'm just—finding it all very difficult." Her voice broke.

I was sorry for her, but I wanted her to leave, so I could start my appointed rounds. "Why don't you try to get some rest? Sounds like you're going to be busy."

Her shoulders straightened. "Right. Thanks." She offered me a tentative smile, the first directed wholly at me. "I appreciate it."

Nevertheless, she lingered a moment more, staring through the chain-link, and I knew if I hadn't been standing there she would have opened the fence to find out what Nelson had been doing.

As it was, she got into her car and drove away, and I went into the house to call Drake. For once he was in his office.

"Don't talk to the reporters," he said when he heard my voice. "Say, 'No comment.' That's the only safe thing."

"They're not here anymore. But Nelson was." I described the little scene I'd just witnessed.

"Nothing in this case is uncontaminated," he snarled through the phone line. "Now I'll have to pull Rucker off of questioning the neighbors and looking for your odoriferous buddy to go and stand by the fence doing nothing." His voice turned speculative. "Don't suppose you could—"

"I've got to go haul a million children around. And you told me to stay out of it, if you'll recall."

"Obviously I didn't know what I was saying." Drake sighed. "Can you stick around until the uniform gets there?"

"Not really." I looked at the clock. School would be out in three minutes. "I have to get moving."

"Well, thanks for telling me. I guess." Drake sighed again.

"Why don't you just haul everything out of there, anyway? Then we wouldn't have to have a chain-link fence bringing down the tone of our neighborhood."

"I'm working on it." He sounded harassed. "We're still understaffed here."

"Too bad. I have to go."

"Thanks for nothing. I'll see you this evening. What are you having for dinner?"

"Whatever I can find." I hung up before he could deafen me with his sighs.

Barker jumped into the Suburban and settled into the front seat. I revved up the big engine, backed carefully down the drive, and inched through the maze of heavy machinery, thunking over the plates they used to cover their trenches. Stewart waved as if he wanted me to pull over, but I pretended it was social and waved back cheerily before accelerating. I had no time for all this complicated human nature. I just wanted to keep Bridget's children safe for a few more days before crawling back to my own peaceful existence.

20

I parked the Suburban in Melanie's driveway and helped my charges down. Corky didn't want to go in, but Susana, a ruffled, dimpled dictator, insisted.

Melanie answered the door with a finger to her lips. "Moira is still asleep," she said, shooing the children toward the family room. "She's having a nice nap."

Melanie's house was the antithesis of Bridget's. The living room was sleek, dusted, undisturbed by signs of human life. In the kitchen, vast expanses of granite countertops glistened, punctuated here and there by glass jars and wooden bowls of oranges and lemons. The family room adjoined it, with French doors standing open onto a patio. The boys immediately commandeered a fleet of vehicles sized for riding on—scooters, cars, even a small bulldozer—and began driving around the room, out the doors, around the patio, back in the room.

Melanie leaned against the breakfast bar that separated the kitchen from the family room. "You want something to drink? Moira will wake up soon."

"I could just take her now." I shifted from foot to foot, uncomfortable in that beautiful, sunlight-flooded room. In spite of the children's drawings posted on the refrigerator and an Oscar the Grouch sticker on one of the cabinets, it wasn't the kind of kitchen that invited lingering.

"You can't wake her from her nap yet." Melanie sounded

shocked. "She'll be cranky all afternoon. Moira is one of those children who need their full sleep."

Perhaps that was what was wrong between Moira and myself. Perhaps both of us just needed more sleep. I perched uneasily on one of the tall chairs pushed up to the breakfast bar.

"I was just looking at my old albums." Melanie turned back to the breakfast bar, indicating a stack of leather-bound scrapbooks I had thought were some kind of decorator accent. "We all look so young—so stupid," she added bitterly.

"Are these from when you knew Richard before?"

"Yes. From my other life." Melanie sighed over the pages of photos.

"Have you heard how he is today? I know he was still unconscious this morning." At least, he had been according to Dinah Blakely.

Melanie pulled a tissue out of her pocket and pressed it to her eyes. "He's holding his own," she said, sounding muffled. "That's all they'll say when I call the hospital. Holding his own."

"Well, that's good. At least he's not worse." I inched a little closer to the edge of my tall stool. I wanted to look at those pictures. "So many people have been telling me about Palo Alto in the sixties and seventies. Was it so different?"

"I don't know if it was, really." For once Melanie spoke without the sharp tone she usually employs around me. "That's what I was wondering about. It's why I got out the albums. Maybe *we* were just so different from how we are now."

Corky uttered a cry of victory as he gained control of the bulldozer from Sam, who dove for the scooter. Melanie glanced into the family room, but if she didn't think it was worth interrupting the traffic free-for-all, I certainly wouldn't.

"You were going to Stanford, right? That doesn't sound stupid."

She shrugged. "We were stupid about life, anyway. But we

did have a lot of good times." She turned a page in one of the albums and pushed it toward me. "See?"

I looked at the enlargement that took up most of the page. A motley collection of young people stood on the steps of a house, grinning into the camera. They wore scruffy jeans and, for the girls, long skirts; most of them had long hair and, for the guys, beards. A few of them looked familiar.

"Hey, that's Bridget's house!" I recognized the pillars on either side of the steps. "But the front steps aren't so cracked as they are now."

"Right, Bridget's house. It was a group house then, owned by the parents of one of my friends. We got reduced rent because of that." Melanie shook her head. "When I think of what we did to that place! We had Day-Glo paint on the walls and ceiling, stripes and paisley. SueAnne, the girl whose parents owned it, even painted all the wood trim different colors— purple in the living room, orange in the bedroom."

"You mean she painted over the wood trim?"

"Yes, if you can believe it." Melanie giggled. "Her mom was furious. We almost got kicked out over that. That window seat in the dining room—she had painted all the panels different colors and even put op art patterns on a couple of them." She sobered. "Of course, it was a sacrilege—all that nice fir trim and paneling. SueAnne was tripping at the time."

"You mean—"

"You know what I mean." The sharp tone was back. "Don't act so goody-goody, Liz. You must have seen your share of drugs on the street."

"I saw them, yes."

"But you were too pure to do any, no doubt." Melanie caught herself up short. "I'm not myself today, truly. That was inexcusably rude." She threw me a look, half apology, half resentment. "I don't know why you rub me the wrong way, Liz. You're a nice person, I'm sure, and Bridget likes you. You can't help it that you just set my teeth on edge."

"Do I really?" I had to smile. "Well, you do the same thing to me, so maybe we can just agree to dislike each other."

"Okay," she said. "That sounds doable."

We looked at each other for a moment, then both of us started laughing.

Melanie was the first to stop. "Well, I mustn't get hysterical. God knows it wouldn't take much."

"Richard means a lot to you."

"You could say that." She rubbed the crease between her eyebrows. "He's my ex-husband, after all."

I stared at her, unable to think of anything to say. She looked defiant. "Your policeman, Drake, will probably tell you anyway. I told Bruno Morales, and he probably passed it along to everybody. Richard and I were married at Tahoe three months before I graduated from Stanford. He was going off on a dig with a bunch of other people from the anthropology department, and I was afraid of losing him to this woman—Aimee DiCarlo. Justly, as it turned out." She looked down at the picture again, putting her finger on the face of one of the men. The jutting chin and pale, straight hair marked out Richard Grolen.

"He had a hot affair with her during the dig," she said, speaking as if to the picture, "and when they got back, she just moved in with us. He slept with her in the spare room, although they hinted they would like the queen-sized bed in our bedroom. I ignored that. I tried to ignore it all. I was gone all day, working in the City, and they were together. He told me I wasn't open enough." Her lips trembled. "After a month of that, I just left. Divorced him. Tried to forget I'd ever made such a mistake."

By this time I'd picked Melanie out in the group on the steps. "That's you, right? With the granny sunglasses and the print dress?"

She laughed. There was no amusement in it. "We all seemed to play dress-up back then. I was into long skirts and all that stuff. But let me tell you, after I graduated, after I left Richard,

146

I left those frumpy granny dresses behind with no regrets. The guys liked us to wear all that old-fashioned stuff—made us look submissive or something. When I put on my first business suit, I felt the power of it. I realized what we'd been lying down for."

Somehow I couldn't picture Melanie as a crusader for the women's movement. Inadvertently I glanced around at the honey-colored maple cabinets, at the lovely daughters surrounded by every comfort.

Melanie caught my glance. "Does this look like selling out to you?" She, too, looked around the room. "Not really. My mom did the fifties' equivalent of this, of course. But the difference is, I chose it. I chose Hugh and I chose to come back to Palo Alto and give my children the good life I'd had. I'm doing exactly what I want to do. That's the difference between my mom and me. She did what was open to her, and it wasn't enough. I know what's out there, and I chose this."

Nice work if you can get it, I wanted to say. But even though we'd agreed to dislike each other, I couldn't say it to Melanie. And besides, if she were going to be so talkative, I thought she might as well talk in the right direction.

"So you and Richard were living in that house—Bridget's house?"

"Oh, no." She looked surprised. "We rented our own little bungalow in Menlo Park. Rents were much cheaper then. We both had student assistantships. We got along financially. Ran around with our friends on weekends. We lived together like that for several months before we got married." She pressed the palms of her hands against her eyes for a moment. "We should never have gotten married. It was my idea—I pressured him into it one weekend when we were at Tahoe. He only did it to oblige me, not because of any commitment to me." She spoke eagerly, as if to acquit Richard of wrongdoing.

"But you still hung out with people living in Bridget's house?" I looked at the picture again. Everyone in it looked young, unmarked. I felt I knew more of them than just Melanie and Richard.

"In the group house. Yes." She looked back down at the picture. "That's why I knew about Nado—the guy who disappeared. The one that nice Bruno Morales thinks might be the skeleton under the sidewalk. Nado wasn't around at the end of that final quarter. We thought he was in trouble and hiding, actually. Rumor had it that he'd been seen in Mexico, that he was still dealing from a P.O. box. That kind of thing. It never occurred to any of us that he could be dead."

"Maybe it did occur to one of you."

"Maybe." She rubbed that crease between her eyebrows again. "This is all so painful, so upsetting. I thought I'd put Richard behind me. That he was just a guy in my past, nothing to me." She got a fresh tissue. "Of course, it helped that he left Palo Alto before Hugh and I came back to live, and I didn't see him. Now I realize—"

"You never got over him."

"A cliché not worthy of either of us, Liz." Melanie slumped a little. Her face was pale, and I realized what was different about her appearance—she wore no makeup. "But yes, that's it. It's not that I'm still in love with him, but I'm just—not finished with him, somehow." She threw me a look. "I don't know why I'm telling you all this stuff. It must be because Biddy's out of town. You messed up your marriage, right?"

"You could say that. I tried to kill my husband."

Once again, our eyes met and we laughed. "Somebody else finally finished him off for you last month, right? Isn't that what Biddy said? That cute niece of yours, Amy, was mixed up in it."

"It's over now, anyway."

"I don't want Richard to die." Melanie's face crumpled. She turned away from the family room, so the kids wouldn't see her tears. "I want a chance to clear it all away."

"Is that what you were doing Sunday, in the driveway? When I was getting Moira out of the Suburban?"

"So you did listen." She got up and went to the cabinet with the Oscar the Grouch sticker on it. It pulled out to reveal a trash can, into which she tossed her soggy wad of tissues. "Don't blame you, I guess. And of course you told it all to the police. I would have, too, in your case." She glared at me. "But I would have been up front about overhearing, too."

"Not me." I stood up, ready to get Moira and go, nap or no nap. "I've learned to duck when it comes to confrontation."

"So you're leaving now?" She laughed. "Don't worry about it. I won't push the issue, and since Richard got attacked it's moot anyway. Yeah, he wouldn't talk to me at all. Like we'd never been lovers, never married. Obviously he was hitting on that Blakely woman. And she had no problem with it." Melanie scowled. "That made me kind of mad—that he would flirt with her right in my face."

"But you're not married now, for what—fifteen years? I mean, you're married to someone else."

"I know that." Melanie closed her eyes. "It's just so hard to believe—that someone I've loved could be attacked like that."

"Believe it." My ears caught the sound I'd been waiting for—a faint cry. "There's Moira."

"So you can get away, finally." This time Melanie's smile seemed genuine. "You're not so bad, Liz. Next time, you spill your guts, and I'll listen and offer self-righteous comments."

"Not on your life."

She laughed and slid off her stool. "I'll get Moira. You round up the boys."

That took some doing, since the boys were now reluctant to leave. Mick had been methodically building walls of huge cardboard bricks and then demolishing them. He didn't want to put the bricks back on their shelf. Corky was in love with riding the little bulldozer and protested loudly about

149

dismounting. Sam wanted a turn on the bulldozer and was equally loud about that.

I herded them into their car seats and was buckling Mick's seat belt when Melanie came out carrying Moira. "Did you hear the phone?" Her voice was tremulous. "That was Bruno Morales. He wanted to let me know that Richard regained consciousness briefly. He's been upgraded from critical."

"That's good news."

"It is. I know that." She handed Moira over, and I began the insertion process, getting her to sit in the car seat, buckling, strapping, finding the right toys to mitigate the whole experience. Melanie was so preoccupied with Richard's health that she didn't even offer to do it better than I.

"If he recovers—if he really recovers—"

"Is there some doubt of that?"

"In any head injury there's doubt. You know that." She slung the diaper bag into the car. "Probably Dinah Blakely's sitting next to his bed every moment. If she's not over at Stanford plotting to take over his job."

This echoed what Nelson had said earlier, and I remembered something that had occurred to me then. "I thought Dinah said Richard was a visiting professor. How could she get his job?"

Melanie pushed the hair out of her eyes. "He told me that was the story the department wanted to put around. But they're considering him for an anthropology chair. He was keen to get it, too. Said he wanted to move back to the Bay Area because the sailboarding was better here than in Massachusetts." She choked up again, but then rushed on, leaning closer. "Now maybe Dinah Blakely's in the running for that job. There's a motive for your detective. Make sure you tell him that."

"You can tell him if you want." I didn't care for the vindictive glitter in her eyes. Melanie really had it in for the younger woman. "And he's not my detective."

"He could be." Melanie looked me up and down and visibly

refrained from shaking her head. "You could certainly do worse."

I got behind the wheel. "Thanks for sharing, Melanie. And thanks for keeping Moira and picking up Mick."

"You're welcome." She smiled, a little ruefully. "Thanks for letting me be a total bitch."

"I had nothing to do with it." I put the car into reverse and left her standing in the driveway.

21 _____

I had to wait in the street in front of Bridget's drive-way while the Public Works guys lumbered several big pieces of equipment away from the blocked drive. It was like watching dinosaurs get valet-parked.

Eventually we could pull into the driveway. Stewart jumped out of the backhoe and came running up.

"Sorry about that." He spoke apologetically. "We can't always keep the driveways free every minute. You going out again soon?"

"As a matter of fact, I am. Kids have classes."

"Okay. We'll keep you unblocked." He grinned. "Most of the folks around here aren't home during the day, so they never know we've been parking in front of their drive."

"Well, we do a lot of coming and going in this house."

Sam interrupted, pulling on Stewart's shirttail. "Hey, mister. What are you digging up today?"

Corky writhed with embarrassment. "Don't bother him," he whispered fiercely to his brother.

"Can I sit in the backhoe?" Sam was oblivious.

"Not today, fella." Stewart ruffled Sam's hair and smiled at Corky. "We'll be here tomorrow, though, and if you get out here early, before we start work, I'll see what I can do for you."

Sam smiled blissfully. "I get firsties, okay?"

"Sam!" Corky was outraged.

Sam didn't care. "You hogged the bulldozer at 'Manda's," he argued. "I get firsts tomorrow."

"Nobody gets firsts if there's any arguing." Stewart took the words out of my mouth. He looked at me apologetically. "Sorry if I started something, ma'am. I don't have kids, so I don't know how to deal with this kind of stuff like you parents do."

"Believe me, I don't know either." I looked at the boys. Corky was sulking and Sam wore a "so-there" expression. "You guys take Mick in and get your backpacks put away while I take care of Moira, okay?"

Sullenly, they took Mick's hands. By the time they got to the top of the steps they were all laughing, letting him hang between them like a monkey. I unfastened Moira and picked her up; for once she didn't protest, just sucked her thumb and stared at me as if she were planning a coup.

When I turned from the car, Stewart was still standing there. "Do you know how that guy is doing?" He pointed over his shoulder at the sidewalk excavation. "The crew asked me about it, and I couldn't tell them."

"Last I heard, he was holding his own. Maybe doing a little better."

"Poor guy." Stewart shook his head. "I mean, what a fate. He might end up a vegetable, huh?"

"There are worse things than vegetables." I thought about my little plants, needing someone to love them, mulch them, water them. Even at that, they're far less trouble than children.

When I realized that I was putting vegetables ahead of Richard in my mind, I felt bad. But not for long. After Melanie's revelations, I didn't have a very high opinion of him.

And I liked her better when she was straight with me, instead of treating me to all that holier-than-thou stuff.

Stewart glanced at the sidewalk excavation. "You wouldn't believe the calls we've gotten since this hit the newspapers, from people worried that there are bodies under their sidewalks, too. As if someone's been stuffing corpses around all over Palo Alto."

"It doesn't seem very likely."

"Of course not."

"Were you working for the city the last time this sidewalk was torn up?"

"Couldn't say. We're always tearing up the sidewalk somewhere in town. I've been doing this for so many years I forget the last job before the next one's done."

"But you all don't tear it up anymore, right? I thought for the past few years a contractor's been doing that."

"Sometimes it's put out for bid, depending on how busy we are." Stewart raised his hard hat for a quick wipe of his head, and backed away. "I won't trouble you any more, ma'am."

I carried Moira inside. The phone rang while I was fixing a snack to carry everyone through their various before-dinner activities.

"Liz!" It was Bridget. "How's everyone? How are things going?"

"Great, just great." I cradled the phone between my ear and shoulder so I could walk around the kitchen on the long cord—just as I'd seen Bridget do so often. Again I got the weird feeling that I was channeling her. "We're having a snack now before the boys go to karate class."

"That's right, karate today, soccer tomorrow." Bridget laughed. "You are doing us such a favor, Liz. I know the schedule's hectic, mostly because now that I'm not doing it, I feel so leisurely. It's terrific."

"So you're enjoying your vacation, are you?"

"So much!" She launched into a bright recital of their activities. ". . . and then we snorkeled. I'd never snorkeled before. I kept thinking how much Corky and Sam would have loved it." There was a catch in her voice. "And Mick would love the music—every night they play, and sometimes there are dancers. We saw the Royal Hawaiian Orchestra with a whole troupe doing Island dances—it was fabulous. How's Moira doing?"

"She's fine. Didn't wake up once last night, and has been eating really well." I looked over at Moira, who was using a slice of cantaloupe to draw designs on her high chair tray. "We're having melon now, and PBJ cut into shapes."

"You're doing fabulously." Bridget sighed. "I do miss them, and I worry about them even though I know you're on top of everything. Is Drake still coming over?"

"He's enjoying playing Dad-for-a-week."

"He's always wanted children, you know." Bridget's voice was heavy with meaning.

"Maybe someday he'll get them." I wondered if I could probe Bridget for information about her house. "Melanie had her photo albums out today when I went to pick up Moira. There was a picture of your house with all these hippies standing on the porch."

"Oh, yes. Melanie knew our house before we did." Bridget laughed. "The first job I had when Emery and I moved out to California was for the same company Melanie worked for. It was in the City, and we used to have lunch every Friday in a different restaurant. That child-free life was great! Emery worked in Sunnyvale and we were living there, but we wanted to buy a house in Palo Alto because it had these big trees everywhere and reminded us both of Webster Groves."

"Webster Groves?"

"Just outside of St. Louis." Bridget sighed. "Of course, Palo Alto is really nothing like Webster. For one thing, all the houses were way too expensive. Melanie knew the people who were selling our house. Their daughter was a friend of hers or something. The house was a wreck. We spent weeks patching the plaster and painting. But it had good vibes, and we could afford it." She paused. "We really should have saved our money for remodeling instead of spending it on this trip."

155

"Well, Emery had to go anyway, right? You aren't costing much."

"That's true." She sounded more cheerful. "And the house will stand a few more years, I'm sure. If it could take what those friends of Melanie's dished out, it should be able to take our kids." She laughed. "For a few years after we moved in, people came by asking if so-and-so still lived there, or wanting to buy drugs from us. Emery always said he wouldn't be surprised to run across a few bodies when he was digging up the flower beds."

Luckily for me, Sam figured out who I was talking to and demanded some chat time with Mom. I didn't have to think up a harmless reply.

Instead I could concentrate on cutting the peanut butter and jelly sandwiches into parallelograms and pondering Emery's incredible prescience in the matter of bodies. Except the body wasn't pushing up daisies. Just concrete.

22 _____

THE karate class fascinated Mick. He wanted to sit in the front row of folding chairs set up for parents. Moira was not so fascinated, but she consented to look at the thick cardboard-paged books I found in the diaper bag. She pointed the characters out to me with one chubby forefinger. "Beebud," she announced, mashing Big Bird's goofy smile to the page. "Cookie Mon." She studied a picture of Oscar the Grouch in his trash can. "Dirty," she said with disapproval.

It was the most she'd talked to me since I'd become Temp Mommy. I felt bad because instead of giving her total attention, my mind was circling around the overload of information I'd gotten that day. Too much—about Palo Alto in years gone by, about Old Mackie's cart and Carlotta Houseman's antipathy, about Dinah Blakely's ambitions and Nelson's surprising accusations. And, of course, Melanie's revelation. It was no wonder my head was spinning.

And somewhere in that unbalanced washing machine load of stuff was one important item, something that would help Drake get closer to finding out who was behind the recent rash of sidewalk bodies. If only I could put my finger on it as firmly and exactly as Moira put hers on Bert's face, on his companion's. "Uhnee," she said proudly.

"Yes, that's Ernie." I gave her a little hug. Her solid weight in my lap, her baby warmth, was very nice. I looked at Mick's rapt face as he watched his brothers, at Corky's fierce concentration on the kick and Sam's stolid movements.

"Let me hear you," the instructor shouted.

"Eh-yuh!" The kids let out fierce grunts as they advanced, kicking, up the room. I shivered. It was wrong to live in a world where children needed to learn karate to defend themselves, where they were encouraged to yell and scream if a stranger spoke to them. But was the world worse now than fifteen years ago, when someone had stashed an adversary under the sidewalk?

"Mousie." Moira held up another one of the thick books. On the cover was a little mouse dressed in calico, with a headscarf tied fetchingly around her ears. In her wee paws, the mousie held a tray of cheese and crackers and a cup of cocoa. I started reading it to Moira, but she insisted on reading it to me, babble interspersed with occasional words. "Inna beeeny tutu wordel, de beybato Mousie! Ana goobitra Housie!"

After a little bit of this my thoughts drifted to the perplexing problem of what to cook for dinner. We'd already had pizza, Chinese food, and noodles, which reduced our available choices considerably. I wasn't yet ready to face the Burger King, and I didn't think the kids were up for baked potatoes and a salad.

"Hey, Mick. What's your favorite dinner that your mom cooks?"

He didn't miss a beat, didn't even take his attention away from the ghi-clad boys and girls in front of him, who were now wielding sticks. "Hot dogs."

Gross. I tried to visualize the contents of the refrigerator, which was full, but appeared to contain nothing anyone wanted.

"Dinny gubba wunna bye-bye." Moira read with a great deal of vehemence, more than the bland pictures seemed to warrant. I was reminded of Melanie's face that afternoon as she'd spoken of Richard Grolen, the passionate vibration in her normally tight and self-contained voice. It was a good thing Hugh was out of town for a week. He might have taken a dim view of Melanie's response to her first spouse.

"Ana brntyger vadir demma," Moira said decisively, finally. She shut the mousie book, clapping the two halves together with gusto and trapping my thumb inside. She found my resultant squeal delightful, and repeated the action several times before I was able to get my thumb out. I didn't really mind. It was worth the discomfort to hear her laugh.

The class came to an end, and I still couldn't remember that tantalizing bit of knowledge that hovered just out of reach in my mind. Also, I hadn't yet figured out dinner. I had just about decided on spaghetti when we pulled up to the house to find Claudia's old Toyota parked in front, right behind the caution tape. Claudia sat on the front porch, correcting galley proofs. A couple of big bags from the Florentine restaurant sat beside her on the plastic bench.

"There you are." She put the galleys away and held out her arms for Moira, who went willingly. "I thought you might need some help with dinner, so I brought takeout from the Florentine—that huge tub of ravioli they have, and salad, and garlic bread and everything."

"You're a miracle worker." I took the bags gratefully and led the way into the house. "This is much better than what I'd planned."

Corky and Sam, still in their ghis, jumped around Claudia, trying to demonstrate what they'd learned in class. When she sat down, Mick promptly climbed into her lap, sharing the ample space with Moira. Claudia lifted an eyebrow. "What makes me so popular all of a sudden?"

"You're familiar." I smiled at her. "Everyone's doing okay, but of course they miss their parents, even if they don't say so all the time. I'll just get things on the table."

I pottered around the kitchen, putting out plates, mixing the restaurant salad with some of my greens and substituting my tomatoes for their prefab ones. I set a plate for Drake, wondering if he'd had a breakthrough and made an arrest. I had a shrewd idea that Claudia wondered, too, and that's why she'd brought dinner over.

She admitted as much when I called them all in. "So what's the excitement around here today? I saw some kind of powwow when I went by this morning."

"The jackals of the press, that's all." I glanced at the boys. Corky and Sam were arguing over whose turn it was to do the dishes. Mick tucked into his ravioli, which I'd cut up for him into quarters. Moira's pieces were even smaller; she picked up a morsel, subjected it to a sober scrutiny, then popped it in her mouth. None of them were paying attention, but I still didn't like talking about it in front of them.

Claudia evidently didn't share my feelings. "Did they ever identify those bones?"

At this Corky and Sam broke off their conversation and looked from Claudia to me.

"More ravioli? Have some garlic bread." I hurried to heap their plates, and shook my head ever so slightly at Claudia. "These little pitchers, Claudia. Lots of them."

Corky looked up and down the table. "I don't see any little pitchers." He took a huge bite of garlic bread and spoke through it. "What happened to our bones? Does Aunt Claudia know?"

"No, she doesn't, sweetie." Claudia looked just a little abashed.

"Our dinosaur bones?" Sam reached for the garlic bread.

"Not dinosaur bones, dummy." Corky was scornful. "They were caveman bones."

"Oh, right." Sam lost interest in the bones. "Can I have some more?"

"Eat some salad." I put a spoonful on his plate.

"You're getting very good at this," Claudia said. "Do you fancy the role?"

"Temp Mom?" I grabbed Mick's milk cup before it turned all the way over. "I'm going to need a full week of solitude after Bridget and Emery get back. No way could I be a full-time nanny."

Claudia just looked amused. "I wasn't thinking so much of being a nanny."

I knew what she was thinking of. It was sweet of my friends to want me to have their version of happiness. I wasn't used to benevolent interest in my welfare, and it touched me deeply. However, we aren't all capable of the same kinds of happiness. Sometimes it's just out of our reach, plain and simple.

Barker barked, the front door banged, and Drake came in, following his nose. "You started without me!"

"We saved you some." I fixed his plate while he said hello to Claudia and greeted the boys and Moira. The meal proceeded at its usual high decibel level. Claudia was discernibly impatient to introduce the topic of interest to her, but I managed to keep the conversation away from anything that might upset the children.

We dismissed the kids to watch the end of "Square One" while the grownups did the dishes. Claudia started pumping Drake before the table was cleared.

"Yes, we did get a fix on the bones. We're not saying one hundred percent, but we think it was one of the people who used to live here, and dropped out of sight in early 1978."

"Dropped out of sight. Good way to put it." Claudia brought a stack of plates to the sink. "So did someone kill him and plant him under the sidewalk, or was it an overdose followed by panic?"

"Who knows?" Drake shrugged. "We're going to have to go through the evidence with a fine-tooth comb. So many of the bones are missing, including the rib bones that might have shown bullet or knife damage." He glanced at me, smiling. "Just by chance, a couple of the ribs the boys were using for cutlasses have either rodent chew or knife scratches on them,

161

according to the county forensic pathologist. She's getting some bone guy from the California Academy of Sciences to look at it."

"We were just there." Claudia picked up a dish towel. "We could have dropped them off for you, or something."

I knew what Drake would think of this, so I asked my own question. "Is it true Richard is out of the coma?"

Drake shook his head. "He's in and out at this point. He did come around and even spoke, but he slipped under again. The docs say he'll probably do this for a couple more days. And also that it's highly unlikely he'll remember anything about the attack or what led up to it. His brain scans are better, though, so he might pull through with all his marbles."

"That's good." Claudia sounded relieved. "A nice-looking young man like that—"

"Hardly young," Drake snorted, clattering the dishes into the drainer. "Middle-aged, if that."

"Younger than me," Claudia said firmly. "Why aren't we using the dishwasher, by the way? Just asking."

We all turned to look at the portable dishwasher, which lurked near the sink. I shrugged. "I don't know how to use it. And this works."

"Oh." Claudia patted me on the shoulder. "Technologically challenged again."

"I'm not challenged by it." I handed Drake the last plate. "I just ignore it."

"Speaking of the latest technology, I didn't see Babe in the drive when I went home," Drake said.

"I parked down the street from here—no time to go home. But I should move it now."

"I'll stay with the kids while you do." Claudia brought the high chair tray over to the sink. "Would Moira have a bath here in the kitchen? I would love to bathe her, but my knees aren't up to kneeling by the tub."

"She probably wouldn't mind. This is a big sink." I won-

162

dered about the attraction of bathing a year-old child. During my recent experience of baths I had learned that such children were slippery, making it hard to get a grip on them when they were obstreperous, which was often. And water went everywhere. And they either hated the bath, crying the whole time, or loved it too much to get out, and screamed while you put on the sleeper. The whole experience was overrated, in my opinion.

Drake walked down the block with me—for protection, he said. I didn't argue when he took my hand. We sauntered toward Babe in the tender dusk, our feet whispering and crunching through the magnolia leaves. I almost hated to get into the bus. We didn't say much as I headed around a couple of corners toward my driveway.

I pulled in, and immediately stood on the brakes, causing Drake to brace himself against the dashboard. Illuminated in the headlights were Old Mackie, who'd probably come to retrieve his cart, and an unlikely companion for him.

Nelson, the archaeologist.

23

"**STAY** in the car," Drake hissed at me. He leaped down from the bus, his right hand headed for his left armpit. He doesn't always wear a gun, but I knew he usually did during an active investigation.

I hate guns. I know how using one can make you feel that you're in control of things for the moment. But it can't keep you in control. And when, eventually, you have to put the gun down, you generally have a much bigger mess to deal with than you did before you picked it up.

I turned off the engine, and the headlights went off, too. "Damn it—" came Drake's voice. I turned the key back on to get the illumination back. Nothing had changed in that brief second. Old Mackie still gaped toward me, his every wrinkle and bit of stubble vividly shadowed. Nelson's expression mirrored his, but for a moment the young man had seemed vested with an odd kind of authority over his elderly companion.

Then they straightened, turning away from each other, facing toward the bus. Old Mackie had his hands in the air already. Nelson's slowly inched up.

Drake spoke. "Please step away from the cart. I'm a police officer. Please stand very still. Liz, do you have a flashlight?"

There was one in the glove box. I pulled it out and got down from the bus myself, aiming the flashlight's beam at the two men. I could just glimpse Drake from the corner of my eye, on the other side of the bus. He spoke into his cell phone, and kept his other hand close to his armpit, ready to draw his gun. I was glad he wasn't waving it around. The situation, although interesting, seemed relatively innocuous.

"Okay, Bruno's on his way," he said, stuffing the cell phone back in his jacket pocket. "We'll wait for the backup."

"What's the big deal?" Nelson tried some bluster. "We're just having a friendly conversation. I wasn't hurting the old dude or anything."

"Is that true, Mr. Mack?" Drake knew Old Mackie, not just because he dropped by to visit me occasionally, but because all the chronic street people are well known to the police. The cops know the difference between the real down-and-outers and the professional panhandlers who make decent money cashing in on yuppie guilt.

"It's true!" Nelson insisted. "Tell him!"

Old Mackie looked bewildered. "Dunno nuttin."

"Look, he was getting into her garage!" Nelson's glasses flashed as he looked from one to the other of us. It would be a clash of lenses when he and Drake made eye contact. Drake would get the better of it. He always did.

"If you insist on talking now, Mr. Drabble, I must warn you of your rights."

"I don't need my rights." Nelson looked pale in the flashlight beam, but resolute. "This is nothing more or less than an innocent chat. I was passing by, I saw this old man in Mrs. Sullivan's drive—"

"Not Mrs. Just Liz is fine."

"Whatever." Nelson went on doggedly. "Anyway, I knew it was her driveway, and I wondered why he was getting into her garage, that's all. I was being a good citizen. I'm not the one you should be arresting."

"I'm not arresting anyone right now." Drake's voice was mild. "Is what he says true, Mr. Mack?"

The bewilderment was replaced by cunning on Old Mackie's

face. "Getta my schoppun cahrt," he said, and spat politely to one side.

A cruiser pulled up across the end of the driveway. Living so close to downtown, where the police have their headquarters, gives you quite an advantage in response time.

The uniform, a buffed young woman, gave me a glance, then obeyed Drake's instructions and frisked Nelson and Old Mackie. Bruno arrived. I turned off my flashlight and got the keys out of the bus—the uniformed cop had her flashlight on our malefactors, and I saw no sense in wearing down Babe's battery. I turned on the outside lights and worried that Claudia would get restive.

Finally the uniform went away, and the rest of us went into Drake's kitchen, after a discussion between Drake and Bruno over whether we should all go downtown or not. Bruno pushed for clearing it up right then and there, arguing that it didn't look serious. Drake wasn't too pleased to welcome Old Mackie into his house, but he did. Nelson was invited to tell his story again.

"That's all I was doing," he insisted stubbornly. "I just happened to see a possible burglary in progress and tried to do my duty."

"Why didn't you find a phone and call us?" Drake leaned back in his chair, his eyes straying longingly toward his espresso machine.

"It might have been over by the time you got there." Nelson wiped his forehead on his sleeve. He turned to me. "I didn't know he was a friend of yours."

"Did he tell you so?"

"Yeah, he said you told him he could store something in the garage."

"Is that true, Ms. Sullivan?" Drake turned to me. Bruno was writing away on his laptop. We were being formal for the record.

"It's okay with me if he stores his cart in the garage." I couldn't figure out exactly what stand to take here. On one hand, no point in getting poor Old Mackie into trouble he couldn't get himself out of. No matter how bad it was for him to sleep under a bush at the creek, I was sure that being locked up would be worse. Freedom is more important to some people than three squares a day and a lumpy iron bed. "But maybe next time he could tell me ahead of time so I know to open the door for him."

Drake looked at Old Mackie. "Do you understand?"

He nodded, clutching the topmost of his scarves in his hands. "Yesshir."

I was still impressed with Nelson's ability to understand what Old Mackie was saying, which had always been a problem for me. "What else did you talk about?"

"What?" Nelson swiveled around and stared at me. Drake stared, too. Bruno just smiled.

"You can understand Old Mackie pretty well, it seems. Looked to me like you were—questioning him or something. Not accusing him of stealing, but asking for information."

Drake leaned back in his chair, folded his arms over his chest, and tried not to smile. "Answer the question. It's a good one."

"I don't know what you mean." Nelson squirmed a little. His round face grew shinier. He took off his glasses and cleaned them nervously on his grubby shirttail. Denuded, his eyes were small and squinty.

"Did you know we were looking for this man?" Drake gestured toward Old Mackie, who blinked. The sour smell of stale beer and cheap wine came off him in waves.

"How would I know that?" Nelson put his glasses back on and radiated innocence. "Look, everything happened just as I told you."

"Where were you yesterday morning?" Bruno asked the question gently.

"I was at home, getting ready to dig. Only we didn't, because Dr. Grolen was hurt and you sent us away."

Drake stared at him for a minute, with Nelson getting jumpier every second. A look passed between Drake and Bruno. "Okay, you can go." Drake pushed back his chair.

Nelson jumped as if jet-propelled. "Okay. See you."

"Wait. You must not leave town. Call me if there's anything you want to tell me." Bruno gave Nelson one of his cards, and a liquid look of concern. "You must hold yourself available if we should wish to speak with you again."

"Okay. Fine. Whatever." Nelson was out of the door, before he'd even stopped speaking.

Drake turned to Old Mackie. "Why did you put your cart in the garage? Why did you disappear?"

Old Mackie stared at him, blinking slowly. Then he looked at me and gave a helpless shrug.

"You were afraid. Tell them about it." I knew I wasn't supposed to speak, that I could say the wrong thing and invalidate the whole interview for police purposes. But Old Mackie looked so pitiful, so in need of help.

After a long moment of silence, Old Mackie suddenly began talking. "Cdn't rully see. Jush a—" he drew quavering shapes in the air with his dirt-blackened fingers— "blur. Shun in me eyes." He held one hand up in front of his bleary eyeballs. "Dint look good."

Bruno wrote all this down. Drake turned to me.

"I don't always know what he's saying—guess we should have kept Nelson around. He didn't seem to have trouble communicating." I got up and fetched Old Mackie a glass of water. It wasn't what he preferred to drink, but Drake took a dim view of handing out liquor during his questioning.

Bruno showed me his laptop screen. "That's what I thought, too," I said. "All he saw were blurry shapes, because the sun was in his eyes. But he felt the shapes were up to no good."

Old Mackie nodded eagerly. "Whammo!" He pantomimed picking up a heavy object, bringing it down on something. "Laidem flat."

Perhaps because I'd been around Moira so much lately, I felt that I was understanding Old Mackie better. "Did he see you?" I copied his pantomime movement. "The man who hit?"

Old Mackie shrugged. "Dunno. God oudda dere, doh."

Drake tried without success to pin him down further, but Old Mackie became distressingly vague about how he'd come to leave his cart in my garage, and what his future plans were.

"You're still in danger, if you were before," Drake argued. "Let us give you some protection."

"Noshure." Old Mackie got up. "I godda go."

After a moment's hesitation, Drake let him go. I called Claudia to tell her we were detained. She had that blend of speculation and avidity in her voice that let me know what she thought we were up to.

I offered to leave, but Bruno said no. "We don't know enough in this case to have any secrets. Perhaps you know something we don't."

Drake nodded reluctantly. He hated having me involved in his work. I wasn't wild about it, either. But I did want all this cleared up. It was Tuesday evening. Friday night Bridget and Emery would be back. It had to be resolved before then.

We sat around for a little while, hashing things out. "It doesn't make sense," Drake said, "for Nelson to be accosting Old Mackie unless he knew the old man saw something of Richard Grolen's attack."

Bruno nodded. "If he was the attacker, he would be afraid the old man had seen him."

"But would he just talk to him? Wouldn't he find some way to eliminate a possible witness?" Drake jumped up and headed for the espresso machine. "I'll make decaf," he told Bruno, his voice conciliatory. "I just can't stand it anymore."

"In that case, I'll have one, too." Bruno looked at me.

"She'll have some hot cocoa made with steamed milk." Drake didn't glance at me when he said that, just busied himself with his machine.

Bruno raised his eyebrows. At least he didn't wear the smug look that the other matchmakers around us wore.

I didn't say anything. Let them all think we were doing the funky monkey night and day. It shouldn't matter to me. But with every significant look, I felt more and more boxed in.

"So what made Old Mackie emerge from hiding, when he was worried enough yesterday to go into it?" I turned the conversation, more to get it away from Drake and me than to put it back on the matter at hand.

"That's a good question, too," Drake admitted. He directed a brief frown over his shoulder at me. "I would have gotten around to asking that other question myself."

"I know. I'm sorry. I'll just butt out."

"Your input could be valuable to us," Bruno said with his gentle courtesy. His turn to frown at Drake. "Liz is a very astute observer, as you've noted in the past, Paolo."

Drake set a steaming cup in front of me and gave my shoulders a brief hug. "Very true. I'm just touchy about this one for some reason. If Old Mackie feels safe on the streets again, it must be because he's set the assailant's mind at rest—or thinks he has."

"Or else he believes that not having really seen anything makes him safe."

Bruno shook his head, worried. "That would not make him safe. And obviously his involvement is not a secret, otherwise this Nelson would not have been pumping him."

"You think just pumping? Nelson could have been getting ready to hurt him or do something." I tried to conjure up that flash of the two of them, caught in the headlights.

Drake, too, was thinking back. "Not what I got from seeing them there," he said. "They had their heads together, looked like."

"What's Nelson doing in this, anyway? What's his interest?" I looked at Bruno, at Drake. Neither of them seemed to know. "He wouldn't be in line for any kind of promotion, like Dinah Blakely. Would he have a reason to want Richard Grolen out of the way? And he would have been four or five when the skeleton was buried, right?"

Drake didn't reply. He rested his forehead on his hand, three fingers pressing between his eyebrows, a sure sign that he had a headache.

Bruno pulled his laptop closer and made some notes. "Perhaps he is simply nosy. This is not uncommon."

"It's not very useful, either," Drake growled. "I don't know what he thinks he can find out that we haven't found out already."

"He seems to have located Old Mackie first," I pointed out.

Drake drained his cup. "We're not getting anywhere here," he said between his teeth. "And you've got to get back to the kids, Liz."

"Right." I said good-bye to Bruno and headed for the door. Drake came with me; I'd expected that. He's big on safety, and although the walk from my house to Bridget's is normally the most boring of occurrences, I wasn't sure it would feel the same that evening.

Bruno offered us a ride, but Drake turned him down. We walked in silence for half a block. The vibes weren't sweet and comfortable anymore.

"So what's really bothering you, Drake?"

"Do you think you could call me Paul once in a while?"

I hadn't expected that response, or his surly tone either. "I don't know," I said cautiously. "These things aren't easy to change. I'm used to thinking of you as Drake."

"You're used to keeping me at a distance." He stopped, taking my hand to pull me around to face him. "That's bothering me."

"Seems to me that it would be a bad time to take that distance away."

His hand tightened on mine before he released it. "That's

true. You're being awfully sharp tonight, Liz. I resent that, because I'm feeling pretty muddled."

The roughness in his voice acted powerfully on me. The skin of my hand still burned from his touch. Something choked the speech in my throat.

"I don't like having my life mixed up like this," Drake went on after a moment. "My job should be separate. It shouldn't involve you. Especially after what you've been through."

I felt a Pity Alert coming on. "I haven't been through anything lots of people haven't handled."

"I know that." He pulled my hand through his arm and started walking again. "I wasn't feeling sorry for you, Ms. Independence. I was just trying—to cherish you a little. If that's allowed."

My warmth at hearing this was slightly allayed by the acerbic note in his voice.

"Look, Drake—Paul." His arm tightened on mine, and I rushed on. "I have a hard time with intimacy."

"So Californian." He sounded amused. "Where did you hear that?"

"Melanie said it, or something like it," I admitted. "But it's true. I—don't like being close to people."

"That's probably news to Amy. And Bridget. And Claudia. And—"

"It's different. They give me my space—even Amy, since she's not always here." I didn't know how to say what I wanted to say, without sounding like an idiot. But then, obviously I was an idiot to turn down what Drake was offering. "Once I let you in, I won't be able to draw back. You'll be everywhere, like a flood."

He was silent for a moment. "So you compare me to a natural disaster? I guess that's not unflattering. I'm sorry if I come off as pushing you. I've been trying to show you that I don't want to take over. Just be a part of your life."

"There's something else." I drew him to a stop in front of

Bridget's house, before he could lead me up the path. "Just in case you were thinking—in case it had occurred to you—"

"Spit it out, Sullivan." He was grinning. "If I was thinking we might fix up some kind of permanent bond—well, my thoughts did run along those lines." He peered down at me in the moonlight. "Do yours?"

"I have to tell you something." I wrenched my hands away from him. "You like kids—you're so fond of the Montrose children. Well, I can't have children."

24

DRAKE'S face went blank. Then his arms came around me, crushing me to his chest. "Oh, Liz. I'm so sorry. How come?"

"Don't be sorry. It was my own choice."

I could feel him stiffen. Then his grasp loosened. "What do you mean?" His voice was carefully without emphasis.

"I—had a miscarriage. When I was married to Tony. I was in the hospital for that, so I had my tubes tied."

"You had a miscarriage. Why?" Now there was anger in his voice.

"Drake—don't yell at me."

"I'm not yelling at you. I just wish I could have been the one to blow that bastard's brains out, that's all. What happened? Did he throw you down the stairs? Kick you in the stomach?"

I hugged my arms around myself. "We don't need to have this conversation if it upsets you so much."

"Damn it, Liz." He clutched at his hair. "Doesn't it upset you?"

"It did." I backed a little way down the walk. "Still does, I guess. When I think of what happened, how I let it happen, I feel sick with myself. I feel that no one can possibly have any respect for me, since I let that go on. I feel totally worthless." I took a breath and steadied my voice. "Not all the time, but whenever I think about my life with Tony. And I always will, Paul. I will never be a person that stuff didn't happen to. I will

174

never be able to get back the things I lost with him. One of those things is that I can't, won't, have children."

His arms came back around me again, and I let the comfort flow from him, because I knew it might be the last time he would want to comfort me.

"Lots of people can't have children. It doesn't make you less of a woman." His voice was tentative.

"But if you hook up with me, you can't have them, either. And I know you want them."

He held me away a little, looking down at me. "I just see my friends settling in with their families, how important that is to them."

"Of course you do. Of course you want that. I can't give it to you." I was having a hard time getting the words out. "Even if I hadn't had my tubes tied, I still don't feel capable of parenthood. It's too much responsibility. I'm too—damaged."

"Don't say things like that."

"They're true." I walked past him, toward the porch steps, and he let me go. "You think about it, Paul. This is a good time to step back, step away. Just think about what you're really getting into here."

"You make it sound like I don't know you." He reached out, touched my arm. "I've been living next door to you for nearly a year now, Liz. I know you." His fingers turned me, gently. "This is big news that you've given me. But it couldn't change my feelings for you."

"Just take a few days or weeks to digest it." I glanced toward the house. Claudia pulled the curtain aside in the living room window; her dark bulk peered out at us. "Don't let all our well-meaning friends push you into something because they want to see me settled. I can take care of myself. In fact, I like it that way."

"I know. You're your own worst enemy, and mine, too." He sighed and let his hand fall. "I have to go back. Bruno wants to go over stuff, and there's paperwork to do. But I'll come over later. I've got the key."

I stood on the bottom step, and Barker began his doorbell act from behind the front door. "You see," I told Drake, "I have Barker to protect me."

Drake made a sound between a laugh and a groan. "Liz—" Without finishing, he turned and walked away. I went on up the steps and into the house.

"So is Drake getting all domestic from his little stint here as surrogate daddy?" Claudia hardly waited for me to get in the door before she pounced on me.

"Not exactly." I was in no mood to be subjected to more matchmaking innuendo. "He has police work to clear up, Claudia. He's too busy to make time with me. And I am trying to be the moral preceptoress of four young, impressionable children. Not trying to seduce him."

She drew back. "I wasn't trying to imply—"

"I'm sorry." It didn't improve my mood to be snapping at one of my friends. "I just don't like the way everyone pushes me to have a fling with Drake."

"Nobody's pushing you," Claudia said, patting me on the arm. "Or at least, we don't mean to be." She hesitated. "Don't tell me if you'd rather not, but why don't you want to have a fling with Drake? He's cute, available, and lusts after you."

"That should be enough, I know."

She grinned. "More than enough for nine out of ten people."

"That makes me feel so special." I appreciated Claudia's unusual restraint—usually when she's curious about anything, she just bludgeons away with her questions until the victim, in sheer self-preservation, coughs up the goods. "I don't not like Drake, but I'm not cut out for flings, and he deserves someone more—domestic—for anything long-term."

Claudia made a rude-sounding noise, somewhere between a snort and a sniff. "Balls. He's lucky to latch onto someone like you, and he knows it. Otherwise, why has he hung around with so little encouragement from you?"

"Claudia—"

"I know. I should just butt out."

"Yes." I looked around the living room. It was surprisingly neat, all the toys put away in the baskets. The two older boys sat together on the couch, their heads together over a book. Mick was slumped in the easy chair, sound asleep. There was no sign of Moira.

"Bridget called." Claudia returned to the attack. "I told her you and Drake went over to your house and hadn't come back yet. We discussed the whole situation and agreed you two were perfect for each other. That's all I'm going to say."

"You just don't know." I shook my head wearily, but I didn't want to go into the details of my sewn-up fallopian tubes. It had been hard enough to deal with then, more than ten years ago, when the whole wretched experience had happened. I didn't want to keep recalling that time if I could avoid it. "Listen, do Drake and me a favor. Let us work things out our own way. If possible, I'd like to remain friends with him."

Claudia looked interested, but had mercy on me. "So did you find out any more from him about the case?"

"That's what took so long." I told her about the strange sight of Nelson in consultation with Old Mackie, and we puzzled over it for a few minutes while Corky and Sam finished up *The Illustrated Encyclopedia of Sharks and Whales*. I picked up Mick, marveling at how heavy such a relatively small person could be, and how luxuriously boneless was his sleep. He snuggled into his bed with a contented sigh, and I pulled the covers up over his square little shoulders. Sam didn't object when I tucked him in, too, and even Corky accepted my smoothing the covers, and one more smooth on those flaming curls. I turned out the light in the boys' room and stood for a moment in the doorway of Moira's room, listening to her even breathing. I liked the comfy feeling that they were snug for the night. I just didn't like being responsible for their continued well-being in the face of danger.

Claudia wasn't ready to go home just yet. She got herself another bowl of the Peninsula Creamery ice cream we'd had for dessert and made herself comfortable on the couch. I knelt in front of the CD player. It had just occurred to me that music was one of the luxuries I'd done without for a long time. Most of the music in the square plastic boxes was unfamiliar to me. In spite of not wanting to deal with the past, I found myself reaching for Joni Mitchell's *Court and Spark* and awkwardly loaded it into the machine.

The first notes transported me back, as music can, and I was twenty, falling in love. With an effort, I put the music in the background, where my past should have been, and tried to listen to what Claudia was saying.

"If only we knew more about the first body," she fretted.

"The only body. Richard looks like he's pulling through."

"He won't be the same. No one is after a head injury like that." Claudia sounded pessimistic. "He might qualify as a walking body. At any rate, if we knew more about the first guy, we might get a handle on all this."

"They know who he is, anyway." I leaned back farther in my chair, suddenly exhausted by everything that had happened in that eventful day. "Maybe he's in Melanie's picture. We could ask her to bring the album over."

Claudia wanted to know about the picture, and I went ahead and filled her in on Melanie's surprise relationship to Richard. This was a tidbit sufficient to distract her from everything else.

"Actually married! That must mean something." The wheels turned visibly behind Claudia's furrowed brow.

"You know, all this doesn't have to be related. The skeleton and the attack on Richard, I mean. Richard could have been dotted by someone from his excavation team—"

"A disgruntled past-al worker?" Claudia guffawed.

I suppressed my own smile, with difficulty. "You're de-

178

tached from this, so you can treat it academically, Claudia. Melanie is not very amused by what's happened."

"I'm sorry. It's rotten of me, of course. A stress reaction," Claudia said hopefully. "I crack bad jokes when I'm under the gun."

"You're not under the gun here."

"Of course I am. I'm going to figure it out while Drake runs around town with his nose to the ground, looking like a blood-hound on a bad-hair day."

I felt immensely more tired. "Personally, I vote for letting Drake get on with it, and getting some sleep ourselves. The kids are up early, you know."

Claudia ignored this. "You said something about a picture?"

"People from the seventies. Standing around on the front porch of this house. Melanie and Richard are in it, and a bunch of others. It's in an album—maybe lots of pictures from that time. You should go over and ask her to show it to you."

Claudia rushed to the telephone. I leaned my head back and closed my eyes, hoping the music would wash away all the tensions. "I was a free man in Paris," Joni sang, somewhat inaccurate as to gender.

"She's bringing it over here," Claudia announced. "I knew you wouldn't want to be left out. And I told her to bring her journal, too. Maria's there to stay with the kids while Melanie's out."

"Journal? She didn't show me a journal."

"But I knew she would have one from that year." Claudia wore her look of triumph. "We took a workshop a while ago, and she said in that prissy voice of hers that she'd been keeping a journal since she was in eighth grade."

"Drake would like to see it, I bet." I suppressed a yawn.

"She'll never show it to him or anyone, but she might tell us the relevant parts." Claudia leaned closer, peering at me. "You're looking very tired, Liz."

"Yes," I said. "Yes, I am tired."

"You should get right to bed after Melanie leaves. Don't sit up late reading."

"Thanks, Mom."

She smiled sweetly at me. "Your welfare is important to me, dear."

Then she fell into an abstraction, and I closed my eyes again, trying to think of nothing more weighty than what CD to put on next.

25 _____

THE music was nearly over before Melanie arrived. She clacked in on her wooden clogs, her loose linen jacket and pants just wrinkled enough for fashion, but not enough to suggest frowziness. She clutched the leather-bound album and glared at Claudia.

"Why'd you have to drag me over here like this? I'd just poured my glass of wine!"

"I didn't drag you," Claudia protested. "You wanted to come. And you can have wine here, right, Liz?"

"I guess. There must be some somewhere."

This didn't mollify Melanie. "You know you forced me to come here by implying that Richard put poor old Nado under the sidewalk. That's total bull." She shook the album at Claudia. "Richard never did anything of the sort! He wasn't even living here when Nado disappeared. He lived across the street, and then we moved to Menlo Park together, so he was busy. I would have remembered if my boyfriend had slipped out in the night to dig holes in the sidewalk!"

"You were in love with the guy. You wouldn't have noticed if he'd dug holes in the living room, probably."

"And another thing," Melanie raged on, ignoring Claudia's interruption. "I did not bring my journal. My journal is a very private document. Before I show it to you or anyone, I would burn it!"

Before Claudia could return fire again, I got up and yanked

181

the front door open, letting in the fresh, cold night air. "Melanie, Claudia, if you want to shout, please go outside where the police can come and make you shut up. Don't do it in here where babies are sleeping!"

Caught in mid-tirade, both of them looked sheepish. In the resultant quiet, we could hear Moira's soft, pre-wail noise. Melanie reverted instantly from irate harpy to mom. "She'll go back to sleep if we just talk quietly," she said, her ear still cocked to the bedroom. "Maybe we should go into the kitchen."

Claudia found some merlot. With the album open on the kitchen table, we hung over it in silence while Claudia paged through. The usual pictures of twenty-somethings having fun at the beach, at the park, in Bridget's house and others', at parties and one-on-one. The people had long hair and long sideburns and Afros and granny glasses and bell-bottoms and long pointed collars on their shirts. I could recognize Melanie in the pictures, but not because she looked like her current self.

Richard was easier to correlate. He had the same jutting chin, although obscured with a beard in some pictures, the same hair pulled back in a ponytail, only with a hairline much closer to his eyebrows than it currently was.

"Who's this?" Claudia put a finger on a man standing off to the side of the group on the steps of Bridget's house, the man who'd looked familiar to me that afternoon.

"I don't remember." Melanie glanced at the face almost lost in enormous sideburns, the wealth of dark curls. "Although somehow I associate him with Mondale."

"I've seen him somewhere." Claudia studied the picture. "Yes, and that fellow beside him, too. The lanky one."

"I thought the same earlier." I looked again at the other man, who had a long chin and alert eyes that belied his sleepy smile.

"I read somewhere that ears don't change. That's how they identify people after a long time." Melanie offered this tidbit. "Oh, there's Nado."

We turned our attention to a picture on the opposite page. After a moment, I realized it was the Baylands, with the interpretive center in the background, looking much newer, not yet covered with bird shit. Some people played Frisbee in the nearby parking lot, while a group closer to the camera watched a couple of men adjust homemade sailboards for launching. One of the sailboarders was Richard. The other one was the lanky man from the previous picture.

"Skipper," Melanie said suddenly. "We called that guy Skipper because he loved the water. Richard and he used to be out at the Baylands often." She put her finger on a grinning, shirtless man, a step back from the action at the boat ramp, who lifted a cigarette to his mouth. Not a cigarette—a joint.

"That's Nado," Melanie said, tapping her fingernail on the joint. "He always had whatever you wanted." A slight note of regret sounded in her voice. "He wasn't a very nice person, but he came to all our parties."

"How can you remember so clearly when he disappeared?" Claudia was faintly skeptical.

Melanie caught that. She hesitated a moment. "I did look through my journal for that year after you left today, Liz. I didn't want the police to know I had it." She cast me a resentful look. "I guess there's no chance of that now. I was looking for something about this incident—Richard mentioned it Sunday evening, after the fight."

"It wasn't a fight," Claudia said. "Just ceremonial posturing by the males."

Melanie threw her a look. "Whatever. My journal is very personal; it's mostly about Richard. I wouldn't want to show it to anyone. Hugh might not—understand." Melanie was blushing. Like me, Claudia was probably seized with a strong desire to read that journal. "I did mention some of the other things that were going on. One of them was this incident."

"What incident?" Claudia demanded.

Melanie took a deep breath. "Nado sold some PCP, or

MDM, or one of those initial things—I don't really remember because I never did that stuff. But a couple of the guys did it, and one of them ended up a vegetable. I mean, his brain was fried. Nado said it wasn't his fault, but it turned out he'd cut the PCP, and whatever he cut it with caused this kid to have a stroke or something. He was mentally impaired for quite a while—I don't know how long, or if he eventually died." Melanie shivered. "I do remember some people cleaned up their act after that, though. And when we didn't see Nado anymore, we just assumed he was ashamed of himself or had gotten busted or something."

We looked at the pictures, quiet for a moment. "Which one is the boy who had his slate wiped clean?" Claudia said.

Melanie shrugged. "I hadn't written down the name, and at this point I don't remember. Richard was my main concern—and Aimee." She pointed out a willowy, exotic-looking girl among the Frisbee players. "She's the one he went off on the dig with, and then wouldn't give up when he came back." She looked at the picture with loathing. "Now if it had been her body under the sidewalk, you could write me down as a suspect."

I sat back and had a sip of merlot, trying to put it together. Parts of the story seemed to overlap, like watching a movie I'd seen before, so long ago that I'd forgotten most of it.

Or else I was having déjà vu.

Claudia started to say something, then cocked an ear. "Is that one of the boys crying?"

We all listened to the roaring that grew gradually louder.

"It's coming from outside," Melanie said. It was pretty loud. I ran to shut the doors into the kids' rooms, to keep it from waking them. Claudia and Melanie went to look out the window in the front door, and I joined them there.

"It's the Public Works people," Melanie said indignantly. "I'm going to complain about this. They can't operate heavy machinery at this time of night. It's against the noise ordinance."

184

She marched over to her purse, pulled out a cell phone and a little black calculator-sized object, a personal digital assistant, then perched on the couch to punch its keyboard. Claudia kept looking out the window, her brows drawn together in thought.

"They do sometimes move the equipment around at night, to avoid heavy traffic," she said, "but that's not what this guy's doing."

"What do you mean?" I craned to see better out of the front door window. The machine was one of the dinosaurlike backhoes, with a fanged head on a long neck which could be pointed down for chomping through asphalt. This particular backhoe carried its head high, nodding like an agreeable monster in time with its body's clanking pace. Having brought it down the middle of the street, the driver was putting it through its paces right in front of Bridget's house, backing and turning, beep-beep-beeping, until its head was aimed at the chain-link fence that surrounded the scene of the crime.

"It looks like he's going to drive that thing right through Drake's chain-link fence," Claudia said. "Public Works wouldn't do that. Maybe this is someone stealing their equipment."

"For a prank, you mean?" I shielded my eyes with my hand to see better out of the window. The backhoe pivoted, backed, pivoted again. Its scrawny neck began to move, the toothy scoop wobbling. "Drake will be furious if that's disturbed."

"Call him," Claudia urged. "I'm going to see if I can stop this."

"Claudia—" She was out the door, stomping down the steps, at her most majestic.

Melanie was still wrestling with her cell phone on the couch. I ran into the kitchen to dial Drake's number. "Come right away, bring Bruno, something weird is happening," I gasped, then hung up and raced outside.

Claudia had positioned herself in front of the chain-link fence. She had her mouth open, trying to yell up to the backhoe's cab over the engine racket. I couldn't hear her. The driver probably couldn't, either.

She was an idiot. A brave idiot, true. And I was a coward. I dithered on the porch, wondering whether to join her in front of the chain-link fence or wait around to pick up the pieces.

The backhoe's engine rumbled down to a low growl.

"That's better," Claudia said graciously at the top of her lungs. "You know, the children are trying to sleep. Why don't you come back tomorrow for your work?"

I ran down the front steps, pausing on the walk. "Claudia, move. The police are coming."

"There's no danger, Liz. It's the Public Works—I can see the emblem on the man's shirt." Shielding her eyes with one hand, she peered into the gloom of the backhoe's cab. "Can't this work wait until tomorrow?"

As if in answer, the engine revved, the scoop reared. In the backhoe's weak headlights, Claudia's face was white. She stood, frozen, against the metal links.

From across the street, a man screamed, "No!" and ran forward. For a nanosecond, I thought it might be Drake. Shock held me powerless. Then he ran through the streetlight before swinging up into the backhoe's cab. It was Stewart.

I moved then. The scoop swung at the end of its long neck in choppy, erratic arcs. I ducked low to get to Claudia and grabbed her hand. "Come on. Get out of the way!"

Someone else came around the chain-link fence from Claudia's other side and gave her a push. I assumed it was Melanie, but when I looked over my shoulder, I saw Nelson's round, blank face. He held Claudia's other arm, but he was looking at that wildly swinging scoop. Claudia watched it, too, like one mesmerized.

Between Nelson and me, we got her going, and then she made two great strides and gained the safety of Bridget's front walk.

"What the hell were you doing?" I shook her arm, then hugged her. "You could have been killed."

"It worked in Tiananmen Square," Claudia muttered.

"Man," said Nelson, his thick lenses glittering in the street-light. "She was nearly toast. Who's driving that thing?"

"That's the question." I would find out later why Nelson was there. Just then the major problem seemed to be the power struggle going on in the cab of the backhoe. The cab was unlit. We could see only movement, shadows. Suddenly the engine shut down. In the relative quiet, we heard an argument.

"This isn't the way." Stewart's voice, loud and urgent. The reply was inaudible.

Bruno's car squealed to a stop, just out of range of the backhoe. Headlights illuminated the scene. The car doors flew open. Keeping low, Drake bulleted out of the passenger seat. He must have seen us spectators, grouped on the lawn, gawking at the entertainment. But he kept his attention, and his gun, trained on the backhoe.

"Don't shoot," Stewart called. "This is all a mistake."

Bruno activated a searchlight on his car, and the interior of the backhoe sprang into light: white shapes thickly edged with black shadows. The two men in the cab threw their hands up to protect their eyes against the blinding light. Then the bigger of the two switched on the engine again, and the backhoe began to move.

"It's Stewart," I told Claudia. "The Public Works guy." Then I recognized the other man. "And his friend, Doug."

Claudia had recovered from her funk. She was scanning the scene coolly. "He appears to have lost control of Doug."

Stewart pulled on Doug's arm, trying to get to the controls. Doug's eyes were screwed up against the light. He backed and turned the backhoe deliberately, until it faced Bruno's car.

And Paul Drake, standing in front of it. Just as Claudia had. Only Drake had a gun.

Stewart lunged at Doug, pushing him out of the driver's

seat, and once more the backhoe clanked into quiet. In the silence, Barker's frenzied yelping sounded clearly. I hoped Melanie was making sure the kids were safe. Like Claudia and Nelson, I was immobilized by the sheer drama of the encounter.

Doug didn't try to start the engine again. Instead, he reached into the pocket of his Public Works shirt and pulled out a gun of his own.

He didn't aim it at Drake. He pointed it at Stewart.

I could hear Drake's indrawn breath, see the way his face hardened. He sharpened his stance, looking for a clear shot at Doug. Drake might have to kill Doug to keep him from hurting Stewart. Drake, too, could be killed. Until that moment, I hadn't actively processed those realities.

Stewart was in front of Doug, preventing a clear shot. Drake circled around. He looked terribly exposed. Crouching behind the car door, Bruno also had a gun out, but his attention was split between the scene in front of him and the cell phone he spoke into in a low, urgent voice. It wasn't clear that Drake could incapacitate Doug before Doug could shoot Stewart.

I began to shake.

Claudia put her arm around me. "It'll be okay," she murmured. Nelson, mouth open, watched as if it were a 3-D action movie on the big screen.

Barker yelped again, and I spared some of my worry for the children. Melanie would keep them safe in my absence. And if I went into the house now, it might draw Doug's attention to the vulnerability of its occupants. There was no way I could risk Bridget's children becoming involved.

Stewart's face was white in the spotlight's glare, but he seemed calm, talking to his friend, directing all his concentration at Doug.

Drake moved a little farther over and found a clear shot. I wondered if he could just shoot the gun out of Doug's hand, as they did in old Westerns. He waited.

Stewart said something more—we couldn't hear it. Doug

wavered, lowering the gun, and Stewart reached toward it. Doug's mouth twisted. The harsh light threw the indecision-sculpted planes of his face into sharp relief.

Then Doug raised the gun again. Swiftly, without pause, he put the barrel against his own head and pulled the trigger.

26

IT was over before we could take it in. One minute, Doug was spotlighted in the backhoe's cab like an old-time vaudeville performer. The next moment, he'd slumped forward. Stewart sat beside him still, his face frozen in horror. The front of his shirt glistened where bits of Doug's brain and blood had ended up.

Drake holstered his gun, ran to the backhoe, followed by Bruno. Stewart leaned over the side of the cab. We could hear him retching.

"My God," Claudia breathed. "My God, my God."

I shut my eyes tight, just ten seconds too late. The picture on the insides of my eyelids wouldn't go away.

"Liz," Claudia said sharply. "Help me with Nelson. He's going to faint."

Nelson swayed, his eyes rolling back in his head. We managed to break his fall, anyway. Between us we dragged him over to the front steps of the house. Claudia yanked him into a sitting position, propped up his knees, and shoved his head between them, as if he were a recalcitrant Raggedy Andy.

"I'm going to make sure the kids are all right." I took one last look at the backhoe. Drake had climbed on the big tires to reach into the cab. Stewart's heaving sounded clearly through the night.

When I opened the front door, Melanie stood just inside, her sickened gaze fixed on the backhoe. She was swallowing rapidly. "What—did he—really—?"

"Yes, he really did." I brushed past her and was almost knocked down by Barker, who whined and wagged so hard there seemed to be two of him. "Are the kids okay?"

"Moira and Mick never woke up. Corky did, but I told him it was some roadwork. Then I heard the shot and came out here—"

"Thanks, Melanie. Thanks for keeping them inside." I stood in the doorway of the boys' bedroom. Corky said something in a sleepy voice, so I pulled the covers up around his shoulders, and he sighed and went back to sleep. Sam in the bottom bunk and Mick in the trundle bed both slept on, undisturbed. From Moira's room came the light whisper of her even breathing.

I dropped into a chair in the living room, knowing I should go back outside to try and help, but not able to marshal my quivering knees to the task.

"What happened?" Melanie came to sit across from me. "I called the twenty-four hour Public Works line, and when I said where the disturbance was, the man actually hung up on me!"

"They might have heard the nine one one calls come in." I gave her a brief sketch of the action, finishing with Doug's blowing out his brains.

She chewed her lip. "So he's the one who did it? Put that body under the sidewalk and hit Richard?"

"It looks that way."

"But why?"

"Who knows?" I leaned my head back in the chair, and felt that I never wanted to get up. "Guess I should make some coffee or something. They might need a place to put things together."

"Right." Melanie brightened. "I'll make the coffee. You tell Drake that the kitchen's at his disposal. After all, if all that other racket couldn't wake the kids, nothing could."

It was tough to make myself go back out there. The street

was alive with flashing lights and vehicles. Inching past Claudia and Nelson, who sat on the front steps like spectators at a sports event, I averted my eyes from the swarm of activity around the backhoe.

"Are the children okay? Did they wake up?" Claudia pulled on my T-shirt.

"No, they're fine. What's been happening here?"

Claudia nodded toward the street. "They're putting the body in the ambulance." We watched silently while the shrouded stretcher slid through the opened doors.

Nelson didn't look good, especially in the flashing lights, which washed his pale face with pulsing reds and blues. "I never saw anyone die before." His voice cracked.

"What were you doing here, anyway?" Despite my impatience to find Drake, to stand by him and know that he was alive, his usual grumpy self, I was consumed with curiosity over Nelson's role.

"I wasn't doing anything." Nelson shrank away a little. "Just—watching."

"Nelson thought something fishy was going on with Dr. Blakely," Claudia explained. She has a soft spot for young academics, even unprepossessing ones. "He heard what Richard said to Melanie—and I must say," she interrupted herself in a voice thick with grievance—"that it was very small of you not to tell me about that, Liz."

Nelson rushed into speech, saving me from having to answer. "I thought Dr. Blakely might have done it—might have hit Dr. Grolen. Because everyone knows she's climbing the ladder. She's grubbing for tenure already, and I heard a couple of the faculty complain that she was barging in on committees, trying to get a power base."

It didn't sound like that cute young thing I'd seen, but I recalled how she'd played up to Richard, just as she'd flirted with Drake. Nelson, at least, seemed immune to her charms; of course, she never used them on him.

"Anyway, Nelson thought she might be after Old Mackie, and he tracked him down to warn him and see if he could find out what the old man saw." Claudia wrested the narrative away from Nelson with an ease born of much practice. "He's been hanging around here, hoping to see her incriminate herself in some way."

"It's not that I hate her or anything," Nelson assured me earnestly. "I just thought it would be cool to find out whatever she was up to and expose her. That's all."

"You'll probably need to make a statement." I moved away. I'd spotted Drake and Bruno, squatting at the edge of the street, talking to someone who sat on the curb facing them.

"I'll make a statement, too," Claudia called after me.

She'd recovered quickly from the carnage. I didn't feel so bouncy. I could still see that picture on the inside of my eyelids, the one with all the red in it.

Drake and Bruno were talking to Stewart, but Drake came over when he saw me hovering at the sidewalk. He held out his arms, and I walked into them.

"You shouldn't have been out here," he scolded, hugging me warmly. "Did you see—"

"Yes." I felt his chest beneath my cheek, the strength of his stocky body within the circle of my arms. "You were taking far too many risks, Drake."

"Wait a minute. That's my line." His arms tightened around me. "It's my job, Liz. Not yours."

"I know." I gave him one last squeeze for comfort's sake, and stepped away. "Melanie's making coffee inside."

He looked undecided. "The kids are sleeping?"

"Like logs."

Bruno came up. "Should we take him downtown, Paolo?" He jerked his head back at Stewart.

"What about the other witnesses?" Drake turned to me. "Who all's here, anyway? Looked like a damned convention on the lawn when we pulled up."

193

"Claudia and Nelson were out here with me. Melanie's inside—she didn't see much."

"All the same," Drake grumbled, "we've got a passel of witnesses. Maybe we should take some statements inside and let people go, not haul this many people down to the office."

"Fine." Bruno glanced over his shoulder at the huddled form of Stewart, sitting on the curb. "He is in shock, I think. Perhaps the EMTs—"

"I'll take care of it." Drake strode off toward the ambulance. Stewart rose slowly to his feet. I found the policewoman, Rhea, at my side.

"Detective Drake says you can show me a room we can use to take statements," she said with a friendly smile.

I led the way inside, closely followed by Claudia, who didn't want to miss a single minute of the proceedings. She dragged Nelson along—he would have been glad to melt out of the picture at that point, I surmised. Officer Rhea was satisfied with Emery's study and started right in with Claudia. I went to tell Melanie that we'd have customers for the coffee after all.

27

DRAKE and Bruno both accompanied Stewart into the kitchen. He sat at the table, cradling a cup between his hands, looking down at the steaming coffee, as if it held the answers to his questions. Without his hard hat, his bent head looked vulnerable, the short graying curls tight around his receding hairline.

Nelson, seated across the table, stared in fascination at the stains on Stewart's shirt. The worst of it had been brushed off, but the dried rust-colored smears were livid reminders of the night's events.

Melanie looked at them, too, but then she watched Stewart with growing puzzlement. Finally she burst out, "Aren't you Fritzy?"

Stewart whipped his head around, staring. "Who the hell are you?"

"Melanie. Melanie Fulton. You are Fritzy!" Melanie sat down next to him. "Remember? I used to live in this house, and so did one of your friends, for a while. You came by all the time to hang out with him. Skipper, right?"

Stewart buried his face in his hands and groaned.

Drake exchanged glances with Bruno. "What basis do you have for this, Mrs. Dixon?"

The leather-bound album was still on the kitchen table. Melanie pulled it forward. "I've been refreshing my memory of that time," she said, with a sidewise glance at me. "And we were just looking at these earlier, that's how I recognized him." She flipped through the pages until she found the picture from the Baylands. The lanky, long-chinned man with the lazy smile and the primitive sailboard. The man with curly dark hair nearby. Both of them not far from Nado, whose bones being found beneath the sidewalk had started this chain of events. Except that it had really started fifteen years ago.

Melanie pointed at the man with curly dark hair. "You're going gray, Fritzy. And you don't have sideburns anymore."

Stewart looked at the picture. But he wasn't looking at himself. Tears came to his eyes.

"That is your friend, is it not?" Bruno looked over Stewart's shoulder. "The one with the sailboard. That is Doug, isn't it?"

Stewart nodded, wiping the tears away with one hand. "Poor old Skipper." He almost smiled, looking at the picture. "He loved to sail. That's how he got that nickname. We grew up sailing together on the Bay. Built ourselves a catamaran, joined the Sea Scouts. Doug invented sailboarding, you know." He said this with such conviction that no one cared to debate the probability of it.

"Doug was the one whose slate was wiped clean." I remembered how Claudia had referred to it earlier.

"That's right." Stewart's shoulders slumped. "We were just partying like guys in their twenties do—beers, drugs once in a while. Skipper got this job with the Public Works so he could fund his sailboard experiments, and I got one too—just meant to work for a few months, through the summer."

"You were acquainted with John Hessman?"

Stewart stared blankly. "Maybe. I don't remember anyone like that."

"You called him Nado." Bruno touched Nado's image with one finger, measuring the inch of space that separated him from Stewart's pictured younger self. "You had dealings with him?"

Stewart hesitated, then nodded when Melanie showed signs

196

of bursting into speech. "It's no secret. All of us bought a little something once in a while back then." He looked at Melanie, and she nodded. "Nado sold Skipper that MDM. I wasn't around that weekend—chasing some woman or other to Santa Cruz, I think. When I came back I found Skipper like he was— just sitting in a corner in his room, almost catatonic." He stared down at the photo of his friend, the intelligent expression, the lazy smile. "After a year or so he got a little better—he could function and all. But he never really came all the way out. He was such a sharp guy, before that."

"You have been a good friend to him, it sounds like."

Stewart glanced quickly at Bruno. "I stuck by him. Stayed on at Public Works at first just to help him out. They gave him his job back, you know, but at first it was hard for him to do." He shrugged. "Never would have thought I'd still be doing this so many years later, but it's comfortable." He glanced down at his uniform shirt, at the ominous stains, and winced. "It was, anyway."

"Why would Doug take his life? What was bothering him?" Bruno was, as always, courteous, interested. But in his own quiet way, relentless. Drake sat back, occasionally making a scrawled comment in his untidy notebook. The way he sat, his shoulders held rigid, told me that he didn't yet see his way clear, that something about the sequence of events troubled him.

Stewart answered Bruno. "Lately he's been depressed. He didn't like working in this neighborhood, where he lived before his life got fucked up."

We were all silent for a while. Claudia came to the kitchen door. Officer Rhea, behind her, looked a question at Drake; he shook his head. She stood there, quietly waiting.

Melanie puzzled over one part of the conversation. "You said Doug invented windsurfing—"

"Maybe not invented," Stewart conceded. "But he had one of the first working prototypes. Don't you remember? You were at those picnics."

"What I remember is that Richard did sailboarding, and I know he took out some patent or other. He still gets money from a sailboard design."

"It was Doug's design!" Stewart sat up in his chair. "Grolen outright stole it from him after Doug's OD because he figured the Skipper would never know. That money would have meant a lot to Doug. And it might have given him back sailboarding. He hardly went at all in the last few years because it reminded him that he wasn't even sharp enough to keep a grip on his own inventions. Just the recognition of having accomplished that would have made him feel better."

"Did Doug know what Grolen had done?" Bruno asked, exchanging glances with Drake.

"Or at least what you say he did." Melanie thrust herself forward. "Richard and I were married at the time. I don't think he would have acted like that."

"He didn't take out the patent right then," Stewart explained. "He borrowed Doug's board—I said he could. Doug wasn't up to using it, and I thought nothing of it. Then a couple of years later when the Skipper felt like boarding, I remembered Grolen never gave it back. He wasn't around anymore, we didn't know where he was. Next thing we know, this company is selling boards based on that design. They told us who they were licensing it from, and that's when I realized that Grolen had just stolen the whole thing. I wanted to turn some lawyers loose on him, but Doug wouldn't do it until just recently."

"He agreed to sue?" Drake sat up, his gaze intent.

"Yeah. He sort of built up a slow burn." Stewart looked down at his hands, then averted his gaze. "When he saw Grolen at the sidewalk that morning, he wanted to take him out then and there."

"So you're saying Doug is the one who hit Richard and left him under that tarp to die." Melanie sounded distraught. "Maybe he was going to come back later and bury Richard—

bury him alive! Maybe the same thing happened to Nado, fifteen years ago!"

Drake and Bruno looked at each other again. Drake was about to speak, but Nelson interrupted.

"He wasn't under a tarp."

We all looked at him, and redness washed over his face.

"So you were there. When did you see him?" Drake's voice was soft. "And why didn't you tell us this earlier?"

"I didn't know it would matter." Nelson ran a finger around the collar of his grubby polo shirt. "I walked to the excavation that morning, and I was early. I'd just turned the corner when this old dude comes dashing past me with his shopping cart full of bottles, rattling away. At first I thought it was because of the recycling truck around the corner. But when I got to the excavation, I saw Dr. Grolen lying there with that chunk of concrete on his head." He swallowed at the memory. "I—couldn't touch him, but he looked dead. And I didn't want to be the one that found him. That's always bad in mysteries. So I—I left."

"You just left? You didn't report it? He might have died, and you wouldn't have helped?" Melanie's voice got shriller and shriller. Nelson shrank a little.

"I thought he was already dead," he said stubbornly. He turned to Drake, who was scrawling wildly, and then to Bruno, tapping away on the laptop. "But there wasn't any tarp over him. He was just lying there."

"Did you see the assailant?" Drake rapped out the question.

Nelson looked miserable. "I didn't pay any attention. I—I don't see so well at a distance anyway. Somebody might have walked away in the other direction. That's all I know."

"Whoever covered Richard up," Melanie insisted, "knew he was alive and wanted him to die, wanted him to lie there undiscovered as long as possible."

"That could be," Bruno agreed. He and Drake were both looking at Stewart.

"I got no comment." Stewart gulped his coffee. He was

jittery with nerves. The silence from Drake and Bruno got to him. "Look," he said finally, "I drive up to the work site, and here comes Doug saying he'd killed Richard Grolen. So I checked it out. I thought the guy was dead, too. I covered him up because dead people shouldn't be lying out uncovered, and I went to my truck to report it, and then that female archaeologist came along and started shrieking, so I knew I didn't have to report it." He stared at Drake, at Bruno. "If you think it's worth arresting me for that, go ahead." He glanced down at his shirt. "It wouldn't be the worst thing that happened tonight."

Then Melanie said, "So how did old Nado get under the sidewalk? Did Doug do that too?"

Stewart stiffened. "I don't know about that. I do know he was upset when the bones turned up. He kept saying they should never have been found."

Again there was silence. I kept waiting for Drake and Bruno to take Stewart downtown for his official questioning. But maybe they were getting a lot more information out of him in this informal setting, with Melanie there to goad him on.

Bruno broke the silence. "Your friend Doug has family here, is that not right?"

Stewart looked stricken. "You're right. I should call. He was estranged from his dad, but his mom lives in San Jose. She'll have to know."

"It's too bad, isn't it?" Drake spoke in a meditative tone. "She'll feel awful that her son not only killed himself, but evidently tried to kill another man and is suspected of yet another homicide years ago."

Stewart put a hand up to his eyes.

Melanie chewed her lip. "But," she said, glancing at Bruno, "I just don't see how that could have been. I mean, it wasn't long after that bad drug incident that Nado was missing. And I remember now visiting Skipper in the convalescent home just before—just before Richard and I got divorced. That was months later. How was Skipper able to get Nado buried under the sidewalk like that while he was in a convalescent home?"

"But you see," Bruno said, "it must have been Doug. Who else could dig a big hole where the sidewalk was to go without causing comment? Someone from Public Works. Someone in familiar work clothes, arriving very early to prepare the area to be poured, who fills in the hole, tamps it down, makes everything nice and normal-looking. Someone who can easily truck away any leftover dirt to the dump. Who else could it be, but Doug?"

Before Bruno finished his summation, we were all looking at Stewart. Drake stood beside him, and when Bruno was done, he put one hand on Stewart's bloodstained shoulder.

"We'd like you to come to the office and make a statement," Drake said, not ungently. "You may want to call a lawyer. You have the right to remain silent. You have the right—"

"Never mind all that." Stewart stood up. He looked around the table, at Melanie's shocked face and Nelson's avid one, at Claudia's austere frown, and finally at me. A smile twisted his mouth. "I knew, as soon as those kids of yours dug up Nado's filthy bones, that it would come to this. I've just been hoping—" His voice died. "Well, not much point in that. I killed the bastard."

Bruno interrupted him, his gentle voice concerned. "You are making statements that may be used in evidence against you, Mr. Corman."

"We're taking you into custody now," Drake said. Officer Rhea moved forward, relaxed but ready for action.

It took moments for them to whisk Stewart away. Nelson rose to follow them.

"Where are you going?" Claudia stopped him in the doorway.

"To the police station. I bet I can just wait there and find out what happens. And if not, I might call up the newspapers. I saw they were interested before. They'll love this." Nelson's face shone with zeal. "I might make enough to stay in school next quarter!"

Claudia didn't move from the doorway. "It's a shame in a way," she said, looking from Melanie to me. "I do think it's important to stay in school. But I'm afraid you won't be able to alert the newspapers just yet."

"What do you mean?" Nelson tried to push past her. "I have a perfect right—"

"We'll go discuss it in the living room." Claudia encircled his shoulders with one massive arm. "These are your options . . ."

The door swung shut behind them.

Melanie roused from her stupor. "Did they just arrest poor old Fritzy?"

"Yes. Looks like he killed poor old Nado."

Melanie sank into a chair. "Man," she said, dazed. "Who would have thought people in our group could kill each other. Why, we believed in peace and love!"

"Things change when you go from the universal to the particular." I collected coffee cups and made a great effort to rise and carry them to the sink.

"I think," Melanie said coldly, "I've mentioned your annoying habit of mouthing platitudes at the drop of a hat."

"I think you did. A word to the wise—"

She laughed a little, but shook her head. "This is just too staggering. And we don't know why, or how, or anything—"

I tried to keep my face totally neutral, but Melanie was sharper than I gave her credit for. "Drake's coming back here tonight, isn't he?" She looked at me closely. "You're going to get the whole story out of him then."

Claudia pushed open the kitchen door, dusting her hands together. "So I fixed that," she announced. "If that little academic weasel says anything to anyone about Bridget's kids or any of us, I'll make it hot for him at Stanford. I still have some markers I can call in over there." She looked from me to Melanie. "What's going on? What have I missed?"

"Drake's coming back here tonight, after they finish up at the police station."

"It could be really late," I protested. "I'm planning to go to bed. The kids are up at the crack of dawn, you know. I need my rest."

"That's all right," Claudia said affably. "You go on to bed. Melanie and I will just sit here and talk quietly for a while. I'm sure Bridget wouldn't mind."

I looked at them, sitting on opposite sides of Bridget's table, where I'd seen them so often before. Claudia looked triumphant, as she often does when she wins an argument. But Melanie's face crumpled.

"To tell the truth," she said, sniffing, "I really need to talk about it. I'm just feeling so overwhelmed by it, by the past and my feelings for Richard, and by this—this violence—"

"But Melanie, you were mixed up in those murders a couple of years ago," Claudia objected. "Everyone in the Tall Tree group was. Don't you remember?"

"I didn't really know the victims that well," Melanie protested. "After all, neither of them was my ex-husband." Her eyes teared.

"Okay." I put on the teakettle and sat down between them. "We'll wait for Drake."

28

"IT was an accident, or so he says." Drake stretched out his legs under the table and sipped the lemon-peppermint tea I'd made, for once without complaining about the strength of its flavor.

Claudia snorted. "Of course, it could have been anything. No witnesses, no way to substantiate—"

"Well, in an odd way, the bones testify." Drake has learned just to break in on Claudia when she gets started on one of her rants about documentation. "Remember, when she looked at the bones, Dinah pointed out that the knuckles had been broken a number of times, perhaps indicating a man who liked to fight."

"Nado did like to fight." Melanie was listening intently. "If we went out to a bar and he was there, we left before the trouble started."

"Well, Stewart says he saw Nado walking down the street one evening, a few days after Doug's OD, and he pulled over in his Public Works truck to give Nado a piece of his mind, threaten him with the police. Nado wouldn't accept any of the responsibility, and said if Stewart turned him in he'd implicate everyone in their group who'd ever bought anything from him."

"That was pretty much everyone," Melanie admitted. "Could have been, well, awkward."

"Nado got hot, wanted to fight. They were standing in the street, right in front of the truck. Stewart knocked him down, he hit his head on the curb, broke his neck. We'll find evidence in the cranium, in the cervical vertebrae, if that's true."

"I thought you didn't have those bones." Claudia sat up straighter.

"Stewart took them. He bagged them up and buried them in the landfill." Drake smiled grimly. "Now we just have to get them back. He's told us where to look."

"So he concealed an accidental death instead of reporting it." Claudia's voice was thoughtful. "Put the body in his truck and covered it up, probably, instead of calling nine one one."

"That was the mistake he made, of course." Drake rubbed the bridge of his nose. "Under the circumstances, it would have counted as involuntary manslaughter. He might have gotten off with a suspended sentence."

"But that sidewalk replacement. Of course he knew about it. He might even have worked on it." Melanie sounded frustrated. "I've remembered a lot more about that particular time than I thought I could. But I still can't remember anything about that."

"And how easy for him." Claudia sounded almost admiring. "He could dig the hole deeper during the day, and no one would say anything. He could fill his truck up with the dirt and dump it, easy as pie. He could tamp it down nicely—it all would look so innocent."

"But he didn't feel innocent." Drake spoke soberly. "Partly he stayed in Public Works to look after Doug, but a big part of why he never got a different job was his need to keep tabs on that sidewalk. He started worrying when it was scheduled for replacement. He offered to do the root pruning, even though it wasn't his usual thing, so he could make sure nothing came to light in there. And he traded for weekend duty so he could be on hand if anything happened. When the work order came in to secure the excavation site, he changed it to a demolition permit."

"It was almost the perfect crime." I swirled the tea left in my cup. "If the boys hadn't wanted to excavate . . ."

"If Richard hadn't come back after so long away—"

"If your Richard hadn't stolen from a disabled person," Claudia said tartly. "If he does recover, I expect him to make restitution to that man's family. Or he can kiss his hopes of an endowed chair at Stanford good-bye. That sort of thievery is still frowned on in the academic community."

"Whatever the reasons, we've got plenty to go on now for making our case." Drake nodded toward the leather-bound album. "We'd like to use that for a while, if you don't mind, Mrs. Dixon. It could be valuable."

"I don't know if I want to help out Fritzy's prosecution." Melanie handed over the album with reluctance. "After all, he had provocation."

"It's difficult to say anything about the penalty phase now, but Stewart's probably not looking at that long a sentence." Drake tucked the album away in his big satchel. "Poor Doug is the real victim here."

"What I don't understand," I began, and Drake groaned.

"Now, Sully, if you've thought up some damned clever reason why we're all wrong, just save it. In this case, we've got a lot of stuff right from the horse's mouth."

"You still have to prove it, don't you?" I silenced him with that. "And I'm sure everything is right. I just don't understand about Doug bashing Richard. I know Doug was mad about the sailboard thing. But what happened?"

"Doug told Stewart," Drake said, "that he had followed Grolen the previous night, found out where he was staying, but he was with some other people, and Doug didn't want to confront him in front of strangers. He went back early the next morning and found Richard just driving off toward the Baylands. Doug was really overcome by that—he didn't go near the water anymore, according to Stewart. He waited for Richard to drive back down Embarcadero afterward and followed him to Bridget's before he tackled him."

"He tackled him? Right away?" Melanie asked.

"I mean, he went up and started talking to him. Grolen just denied it all, and told Doug that he knew the bones were Nado, and he figured it was Skipper's good friend Fritzy who put Nado there. He said if Doug pressed him about the sailboarding royalty, he'd have to turn Stewart in for Nado's murder. Evidently," Drake said, "he was quite nasty about it. He turned away, and Doug just heaved up a chunk of concrete and dotted him. Then he thought Grolen was dead and bolted back to his backhoe. Stewart arrived for work, and Doug told him about it, almost incoherent with fear and remorse. Stewart went and covered up Grolen to buy time before the body was discovered, time for Doug to compose himself. He says he thought Grolen was dead, too. Maybe he did."

"You think he—wanted Richard to die?" Melanie covered her mouth with her hand.

"I think that would have been fine with him, if it never involved him or Doug."

We were silent for a moment, and then Drake stretched, yawning hugely. "And now ladies, I've told you far more than anyone would approve of, so keep it under your collective hats. And don't go messing around with this stuff anymore."

"Don't be so patronizing," Claudia said disdainfully. "If it hadn't been for Melanie, you'd still be fumbling around with this."

"You said it much better earlier, Claudia." I grinned at her. "You said he was sniffing around like a bloodhound on a bad-hair day."

Drake grinned, too. Claudia blushed.

"Well, it is late," she said, standing up. "I've got to get

going. And you should get some sleep, Liz. Those kids get up early, you know."

"Yes," I said. "I know."

"Maria will be wondering what's become of me." Melanie stood up too, reaching for her Coach bag. She glanced at Drake's bulging briefcase. "Be careful with that album, Detective. It's not some cardboard throwaway."

"I'll be careful."

I saw them to the door and locked it after them. Barker, stretched out impossibly long on the living room floor, sighed deeply. Drake echoed the sigh.

"You must be pooped."

He winced. "Please, don't use that word so cavalierly. I'll be afraid Moira is going to wake up."

"They're down for the count, if all this commotion didn't get them up." I hesitated. "Why don't you take Bridget and Emery's bed? I'll make do with the couch tonight."

"No way." He pulled me toward him for one of those almost-chaste kisses on my forehead. "I'd be intimidated by the action that bed's seen. Four kids!"

"It is a little nerve-racking." I put my arms around his neck. He went very still. "You've never done that before."

"Don't be silly. Of course I have."

He shook his head. "Not without prompting from me. Not without me doing it first."

I realized he was right. "Well, then, let's try for another first." I put my hands on his cheeks, felt the scratchy stubble against my palms, and tugged until his mouth was close enough. It felt good to be in charge of the kiss. It just felt good, period.

"Well." His voice was a little unsteady. "There's some other stuff we haven't done yet, too."

"Later, Drake." I smoothed back his wild hair. "Paul. I'm only Temp Mom for a few more days."

I hadn't known before that gray eyes could be so warm. After a moment, he turned away and started taking cushions off the sofa.

"I'll hold you to that," was all he said.

29

MOIRA and I were listening to John Hiatt the next morning when the phone rang.

"Liz." It was Janet Aronson's gravelly voice. "I just wanted you to know that I went to the Senior Center early this morning and spoke to the program director. She's not about to take action on anything Carlotta said."

"That's good to know." I hadn't realized I was so concerned about retaining my class until something tight in my chest loosened on hearing her words.

"So just ignore her," Janet went on.

"Carlotta's going to stay in the class?"

" 'Fraid so." Janet sounded unconcerned. "It ought to be fun, right?"

"Janet, I'm counting on you to set an example in civility."

She snorted. "Right. See you tomorrow, Liz."

Before I could turn the music back up, the phone rang again. "Liz Sullivan? This is Jim Pierce." It was a pleasant male voice. "My mother tells me you're looking for background information on the Palo Alto scene in the seventies."

"Oh, right. Thanks for calling." I hadn't given this another thought for hours. "You know, I don't know yet if I'll be doing that story or not. Can I call you if I do?"

"Sure." He hesitated. "Hearing about that body they found under the sidewalk on the news last night, I really started remembering. Maybe I'll jot some of it down for you."

"Or for yourself. You might write an article before I get to it."

He was quiet a moment. "Maybe. Well, nice talking to you."

This time, I got to hear some of "The Wreck of the Barbie Ferrari" before the phone rang again.

It was Bridget, sounding strained. "Tell me that I'm hallucinating. I'm sitting here in my hotel room, looking at the news on TV, and I see my house with a bunch of yellow tape strung up around the sidewalk."

I glanced out the front window. The curb was thick with TV news vans, pointing their dishes skyward. A ragged throng of media types hovered outside the chain-linked fence, pestering the archaeological team inside the fence with incessant, whining pleas to speak for the camera. Dinah Blakely stood in an attitude of command, shaking her head coyly at all the cameras. I could see her prim lips shaping the words, "No comment." Drake would have loved it.

"I'm afraid you're not hallucinating, Biddy." I turned my back on the media circus and crouched down to hand Moira a stray bristle block. "There's been a bit of excitement. Nothing to do with you and Emery. An old body under the sidewalk, one that had been there for fifteen or more years. It's all cleared up now, but of course the press are making a big deal out of it."

"It looks like a very big deal, indeed," Bridget said, her voice ominously even.

"They don't have any real news, that's why." I cradled the phone between my shoulder and ear and stuck a few bristle blocks together on my own account. "Remember how after the last earthquake they kept showing shots of the same supermarket with all the stuff off the shelves, all over the country? Made it look like all of California had crumbled."

"That's true." Bridget's voice brightened. "So it was pretty straightforward, huh? Old bones, no big deal."

"Right." I ignored the knock on the front door. We were

sitting out of sight on the floor, experience having taught me that it wasn't safe to let the jackals see you. "Still having fun?"

"I was until I turned on the news this morning," Bridget said tartly. "Maybe we should come home early. Or I could come home early."

"Why?" I made my voice sound injured. "Aren't I good enough to take care of your kids when some minor problem comes up? You feel like you can't trust me?"

"No, no. It's not that. Liz, I didn't mean to imply—" Bridget stopped when she heard me laughing. "You don't sound too worried," she decided.

"It truly is all cleared up. And it's interesting. When you get back, after your vacation has run its prescribed course, I'll fill you in."

"I look forward to that." Bridget hesitated. "You sound different, Liz. Almost—relaxed. You like being a surrogate parent that much?"

"It has its moments." I was more comfortable with parenting. But I was also still comfortable with my own lack of wherewithal for parenthood. Being Temp Mom was fine. I would enjoy my solitude at the end of the week.

Or at least, my partial solitude. I had another form of enjoyment in mind as well.

MURDER IN THE MARKETPLACE
by Lora Roberts

Freelance writer Liz Sullivan is on the scene when the body of beautiful Jenifer Paston is discovered. Jenifer happens to be a star at SoftWrite, the Silicon Valley company where Liz is temping.

Liz's neighbor, police detective Paul Drake, advises her to stay away from the crime scene. Unfortunately, freelance writing doesn't pay the bills—so Liz is forced to continue working at SoftWrite, where spite, sex, and greed take top priority, and where the computer games are murder....

MURDER MILE HIGH
by Lora Roberts

For the first time in years, struggling writer Liz Sullivan is headed home to Denver to visit her estranged family. No sooner does she arrive than her former husband's corpse is delivered to her father's front porch with a bullet between the eyes.

Since Liz once tried to kill her violently abusive husband, the police assume she has finally succeeded....

Published by Fawcett Books.
Available at your local bookstore.